Lunatic Fringe

Crime Fiction Inspired by One-Hit Wonders
Volume II
Edited by J. Alan Hartman
****

White City

Press

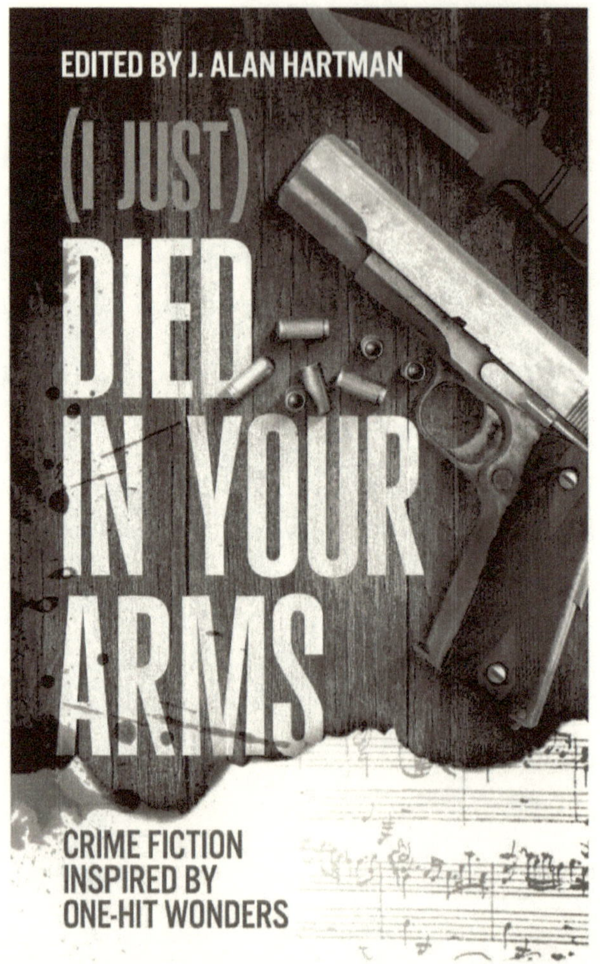

Hitting the charts only once isn't just unfortunate...it's a crime.
Over the decades, tons of musical artists and groups have had a hit song that has lived on long after the tune topped the charts and is often looked upon fondly for decades to come. For some musicians, this may be the only the song they're ever known for and they fade into obscurity soon thereafter. These are affectionately known as "one-hit wonders," and are much celebrated by fans and music publications, particularly on September 25th each year on One-Hit Wonder Day

12 of today's best short story authors have taken their favorite one-hit wonders and reimagined them as the influence for some pretty heinous crimes. *(I Just) Died in Your Arms* features a decades-spanning collection of immediately recognizable hit songs turned into stories from the amazing talents of Vinnie Hansen, Jeanne DuBois, Josh Pachter, J.M. Taylor, Christine Verstraete, Sandra Murphy, Joseph S. Walker, Wendy Harrison, Bev Vincent, Leone Ciporin, Adam Gorgoni and Barb Goffman.

Paperback ISBN: 9781963479027 eBook ISBN 9781963479010

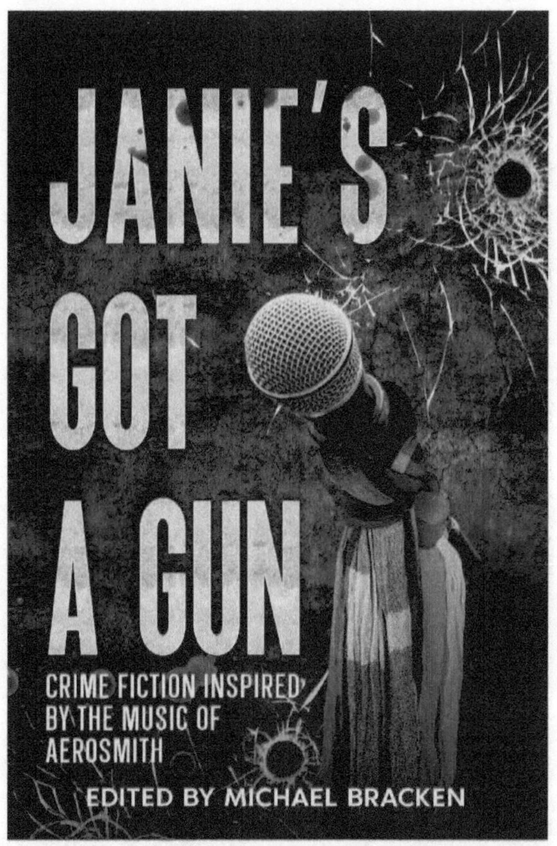

With a career spanning over 50 years, Aerosmith has been a trend-setter in the world of rock and roll. From early hits such as "Dream On" and "Sweet Emotion" to their legendary collaboration with Run DMC for a cover of "Walk This Way" to their contribution of "Don't Wanna Miss a Thing" on the soundtrack for *Armageddon*, Aerosmith has proved time and again to be a band capable of reinvention and constant influence on the music scene.

With their 2024 announcement that the band will no longer tour, 16 crime fiction authors have come together to produce an anthology paying tribute to some of Aerosmith's greatest hits and their studio albums. This literary trip across the rock and roll landscape is courtesy of multi-award winning editor Michael Bracken with stories by Ed Ridgley, Bill Baber, Eve Fisher. Avram Lavinsky, John C. Breuning, Jeffrey Marks, Mary Dutta, Tom Mead, Steve Liskow, Joseph S. Walker, Adam Meyer, John M. Floyd, Leone Ciporin, M.E. Proctor, Tom Milani and Jim Winter.

Paperback ISBN: 9781963479539 — eBook ISBN: 9781963479522

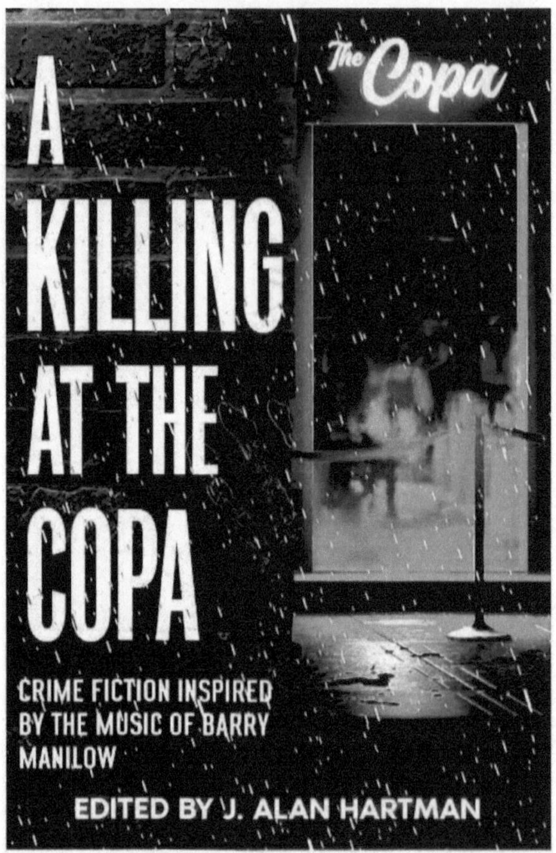

Manilow also created a legendary musical crime in his song *Copacabana*, telling the story of feather-wearing dancer Lola who is caught between bartender Tony and patron Rico as the two men vie for her affections…and ultimately meet untimely ends.

Now, 13 crime author fans of Barry (affectionately known as "Fanilows") take on other songs from his collection of hits to tell all new stories of love, life, relationships and other situations gone horribly wrong. All the hits are here, as well as a few lesser-known tracks.

As Manilow sings, "there was blood and a single gunshot. But just who shot who?"

This collection features all new stories from Karen Keeley, Linda Kay Hardie, Adam Gorgoni, Maya St. Clair, Matt McGee, Laurie Stevens, Caleb Weinhardt, Kurtis Rupé, Recita Clemons, J. M. Taylor, John M. Floyd, T. Fox Dunham, Christine Verstraete and Shari Held.

Paperback ISBN: 9781963479706
eBook ISBN: 9781963479690

Lunatic Fringe

Crime Fiction Inspired by One-Hit Wonders
Volume II
Edited by J. Alan Hartman

This edition published by White City Press
An imprint of Misti Media LLC
https://whitecitypress.com
Available in both Paperback and eBook Editions
1 2 3 4 5 6 7 8 9 10

This is a work of fiction. The characters, dialogue and events in this book are wholly fictional, and any resemblance to companies and actual persons, living or dead, is purely coincidental

Acknowledgements

Say That You'll Be True by Steve Liskow
Inspired by Susie-Q (Dale Hawkins 1957)

The School Secretary and The Cheater by Vicki Erwin
Inspired by The Cheater (Bob Kuban and The In Men 1965)

How Many Teardrops by Kaye George
Inspired by 96 Tears (Question Mark and the Mysterians 1965)

Baby It's You by Judy Penz Sheluk
Inspired by Baby It's You (Smith)

Mr. Big Stuff by John M. Floyd
Inspired by Mr. Big Stuff (Jean Knight 1971)

In the Middle of the Day by Linda Kay Hardie
Inspired by Romeo's Tune (Steve Forbert 1979)

Nothin' Gonna by Sandra Murphy
Inspired by Break My Stride (Matthew Wilder 1983)

Rock Me Amadeus by Karen Keeley
Inspired by Rock Me Amadeus (Falco 1986)

(I Just) Died in Your Arms by Teresa Inge
Inspired by (I Just) Died in Your Arms (Cutting Crew 1986)

Black Velvet by Michael Bracken
Inspired by Black Velvet (Alannah Myles 1989)

Roll to Me by Mary Dutta
Inspired by Roll to Me(Del Amitri 1995)

I Know (What You Did in Pittsburgh) by Nikki Knight
Inspired by I Know (Dionne Farris 1995)

Sunny Came Home by Adam Meyer
Inspired by Sunny Came Home (Shawn Colvin 1997)

Contents

Introduction

Back in January of 2024, White City Press published its second book ever titled *(I Just) Died In Your Arms: Crime Fiction Inspired by One Hit Wonders*. It's hard to believe that the two-year celebration of that title is just around the corner.

At the time, White City Press was in startup mode and we were hoping for the best. We didn't have much scheduled yet for the year, but we had a handful of authors that were willing to let us share their talents with the rest of the world. We held an open submission call for the *One Hit Wonder* anthology, and we received a slew of terrific submissions. People were excited about the idea of writing crime fiction based around those songs where we remember every lyric but couldn't possibly remember the name of the artist who sang it. Even if you put a gun to our heads. Which, ironically, happened in some of those stories.

To say that *OHW* (as it's affectionately referred to) was a success is an understatement. It went on to be an international bestseller, was nominated for several awards both as an anthology and for some of the individual stories contained within its pages, and launched our entire "Inspired By" series that includes crime anthologies about music of the 1980s, songs from artists such as Aerosmith and Barry Manilow, and will have even more to come.

Without a doubt, the question I get asked the most is "when is there another volume of *OHW* going to be released?" We had originally planned on the second volume being released for National One Hit Wonder Day in September of 2024, but it just didn't come together in time. So, we tabled it until National One Hit Wonder Day 2025, which happens on September 25th.

In the end, I'm glad it didn't happen by the original date. Over the last year and a half I've had the opportunity to work with new-to-me authors as well as folks from my publishing past. I've had so much fun working with these folks, that I decided to create my own invitation list of people to include in *OHW2*. All the contributors to this anthology were handpicked by me and my love for what they've written for WCP in the past.

I'd like to thank Michael Bracken for re-introducing me to Adam Meyer, Sandra Murphy for bringing me Vicki Erwin and our resident Canadian Karen Keeley, and Teresa Inge for showing me the talents of Mary Dutta. It was in their anthologies they edited for White City Press that these terrific writing voices came to my attention and are how they came to be included in the pages within.

And, of course, thanks to all of you who read our works and continue to support our authors and independent publishing. Without all of you we wouldn't be celebrating two years of White City Press in November of 2025, we wouldn't have nearly 50 titles published, and there wouldn't be this volume of *OHW2* in your hands.

I guess I'll have to keep all of you happy and come back with *OHW3*. You know, since you twisted my arm.

J. Alan Hartman
Editor-in-Chief, White City Press
September 2025

Suzie-Q
(Dale Hawkins)
Chess/Checker 1957

Susie Q is a rockabilly song co-written and performed by American musician Dale Hawkins, released in 1957. The song was a commercial success and became a classic of the early rock and roll era, being recorded by many other performers in subsequent years.

Say That You'll Be True

Steve Liskow

The summer after my senior year, I mowed lawns and trimmed shrubbery for most of our neighborhood. I had fifteen customers, so I did three lawns a day one week and hedges the next, which left my weekends free. By the end of the second week, I'd figured out when people would be home so I could get paid on the spot instead of having to come back another time.

The last Wednesday in June, I finished the Harrisons' yard about eleven, and Mrs. Harrison handed me an envelope with my money.

"Going to be a hot one today, Dale." She was kind of pudgy and loved to bake, and the cake and pie smells coming from her kitchen made my mouth water.

"Yes, ma'am." My shirt was already plastered to my back. "That's why I'm trying to get through early."

"Good idea." She wiped her hands on her apron and I heard a fan behind her, moving the sticky air around her kitchen.

I crossed the street and saw a plumber's truck in the driveway. When Mrs. Quinn opened the door, my eyes almost popped out of my face. She was wearing a slip, so sheer I saw two dark circles under it. She looked like one of those girls my buddies and I admired in magazines down at Keller's Drug store.

"Oh. Dale." Her chest moved when she breathed. "I guess you're here to trim my bush, aren't you?"

"Uh, it's your lawn this week, ma'am." I heard Elvis behind her. Mr.

Quinn owned Broadcast City, so the Quinns had a record player that fitted into the cabinet with the radio. They had a 21-inch TV, too. I made do with my transistor radio.

"Oh, that's right." Mrs. Quinn crossed her arms and I caught myself staring at her chest. "Um, could you take special care with the back yard today? We're having a few friends over for the weekend and we might play croquet or something."

"Um, sure thing."

She closed the door and I guided the mower to the big back yard. They had four chairs and a picnic table, with a hammock swinging between two large maple trees. I moved all the furniture, but I still had to duck under that hammock every time I made a pass between the trees. I replaced everything and was about to move the side yard when the kitchen door opened and a guy with a tool box walked out. Ed Thome, who graduated the year before me. He had a bouncy walk and seemed to be humming until he saw me.

"Hey, Dale."

"How's tricks, Ed?" I cut the mower's engine and looked at his hands. Clean as a whistle. "You do this for your job now, plumbing?"

"Yeah. Trade school. Good money, and even better hours. You doing this for a company, or on your own?"

"Just me," I said. "I'm saving up for J.C. in the fall."

"That so?"

"Yeah. My mom wants me to join the Army, but I want to try college." Over Ed's shoulder, I saw Mrs. Quinn standing in the doorway in that slip. Ed saw my eyes move and looked back.

"Uh, I better get going. Got other calls to make. See you around, Dale."

"You bet."

His truck eased down the driveway. When I finished mowing, Mrs. Quinn gave me my money. By then, she wore madras Bermuda shorts and a white sleeveless top. The radio drifted out the door behind her again, a song I didn't recognize, but I liked the guitar in it.

"New song," she said. "I just heard it for the first time yesterday."

"What's it called?" I asked.

"'Susie-Q," she said. "Like me."

"Oh, is your first name Susie?"

"Susannah. But Susie's my nickname."

I mowed the Holcombs' lawn, too, got my envelope from Mrs. Holcomb, and reached home before the hottest part of the day. I took a shower and stretched out on my bed with my transistor. That new song came on again, and the rhythm made me close my eyes and imagine Mrs. Quinn standing in the doorway with that slip dripping off her.

* * *

I listened to a few more songs, then walked to the bank and deposited my money. I did that every day so I didn't start spending it on stupid stuff. I didn't have a girlfriend, and that made it easier.

"Hi, Dale."

Fran, from my trig class, smiled across the counter. She wore a bright orange headband and had glasses with little black frames that made her brown eyes look huge. The glasses and her white blouse made her look much older, but we graduated together only a few weeks earlier.

"Uh, hi. Are you working here now?" Sometimes, I'm so brilliant I can't stand it.

"Yep. Started two weeks ago."

I gave her my deposit slip and wondered what else I could say. She typed the amount and smiled again.

"Oh, I've always dreamed of having a rich husband."

My throat dried up. I was outside before I could breathe again, and then I kicked myself for not trying to chat with her some more. I only went on a few dates in high school, and never had a steady girlfriend. I told myself it would be different in college.

On the way home, I turned left and walked past the Quinns' house again. They lived on the far side of the block across the street from us, so it wasn't that far out of my way. My mom was a secretary at an insurance company, and she wouldn't be home for another couple of hours. I went into our back yard and read a chemistry book from the library to get ready for the fall. I had my transistor radio, and that song came on again.

I imagined myself dancing with a girl to that song. I don't dance much, but the music had a beat that made me want to move. I wondered if Fran like to dance. Then I wondered about Mrs. Quinn. Susie-Q. I imagined her walking away from me in that slip again and forgot all about chemistry.

Two weeks later, it rained on Tuesday, so I cut four lawns on Wednesday instead of three. I wanted to do five, but the grass was still wet and kept clogging up my mower. When I walked up the Quinns' steps to ring the bell, I saw a truck in the driveway again. A carpenter, this time. When Mrs. Quinn answered, she was wearing a dress but her hair looked kind of mussed up.

'I wasn't sure you'd come today, Dale. That rain yesterday and all. But you always come on time, don't you?"

Her eyes told me she was saying something else, too. I cleared my throat and nodded. With her hair all mussed like that, she looked even prettier, like she'd been tossing her head around and dancing to that song.

"Well, I'll just put your envelope under the mat here, all right?" She pointed to the welcome mat beneath my sneakers. "That way you won't have to knock again when you finish."

"Good idea."

I put the furniture back after mowing the back yard before the back door opened and a man with another toolbox strode down the steps to his truck. He was a lot taller than me and had big muscles. He roared down the driveway like he didn't even see me.

When I finished mowing, I walked down the side of the house and around the corner to get my money from under the mat. Through an open window, I heard Mrs. Quinn singing "Susie-Q," the shower running in the background. By the time I got home I was tired from all the work, but the idea of Mrs. Quinn taking a shower woke me right up.

By the end of July, I had almost $300 in the bank. That same carpenter truck was in the driveway when I trimmed Mrs. Quinn's shrubbery again, and I wondered what they were remodeling. Their house looked like most of the others in my neighborhood, a two-story frame, white, with green woodwork. The porch spread across the entire front of the house, and Mrs. Quinn had two plants hanging from hooks above the railing, where they got lots of sun. That porch and the yard were a little bigger than some of the neighbors', but that was the only difference I could see.

Fran took my deposit again.

"You come in here every day, don't you, Dale?" She wore a tan blouse that made her hair the rich brown of a Hershey bar.

"I don't want to keep my money home," I said. "I'd spend it, but I'm trying to save up for J.C. this fall."

"You're going to college?" Her eyes got round. "Wow."

"Well," I hedged, "I'm going to try it. My mom wants me to join the Army, but I want to try college first. Maybe join up if I flunk out."

She looked older, almost like a teacher, and shook her head. "I don't think you'll flunk out. You're really smart."

"You think so?"

"I know so." She looked at my deposit slip and the money. "You're saving lots of money and working hard. How do you relax?"

There was nobody behind me, so I took time to think about that.

"Well, there's movies and stuff. And some of the guys still go over to the vacant lot and toss a ball around."

"Sure," Fran said. "And you've got enough money to buy your girlfriend nice things."

I shook my head. "I don't have a girlfriend."

For the first time, I wondered why. My father died three years before. Mom didn't go out for a year after that, but now she went on a date once in a while, usually out to dinner and dancing. She didn't have a steady man, either. Maybe it ran in the family.

"You don't?" Fran looked amazed. She stamped my deposit slip and handed it back. "A good-looking guy like you?"

I wasn't used to hearing that. Especially not from a girl. I thought about it the rest of the day, even when I was listening to my transistor radio. The next Monday, I made sure I was in Fran's line to deposit my money and when I got to her window, I asked her for a date.

"Really?" She blinked and I felt like a stupid little kid. "Okay. When?"

"How about this Saturday?" If I stopped to think about it too long, I'd run out of the bank as fast as my legs could carry me. "We can go to a movie. You can pick it."

"I'll look at the paper tonight. Thank you, Dale."

Mom was amazed when I asked to use the car, but she didn't give me much of a lecture about driving safely.

Fran and I saw *April Love* with Pat Boone and Shirley Jones. We shared a box of popcorn and listened to the songs, and I realized I'd heard "April Love" on my transistor a few times.

We drove back to her place and sat in the car for a few minutes while I struggled to keep the conversation going. Fran was really pretty and I liked being with her, but I felt like I was one stupid word away from ruining the evening. Finally, I walked her to her door and she stood looking at me. I knew I had to say something.

"Um, this was lots of fun, Fran."

"It was, Dale. Thanks for asking me out."

"W-would you like to do something again next week? Maybe another movie, or…"

"Yes."

I tried to look cool. Then she leaned over and kissed me on the cheek and disappeared into the house. I floated back to the car and didn't even remember driving home. I undressed for bed and tucked my earpiece into my ear. "April Love" played once before I fell asleep. So did "Susie-Q."

The next week, Fran suggested that we go to a drive-in. I don't remember what we saw, or at least paid to see, because before the newsreel even finished, she slid over and put her head on my shoulder. A few minutes later, we were holding hands. Her hair smelled like flowers, and she was soft and warm against me.

When the first movie started, she turned her head and her lips brushed against mine. I'd never kissed a girl before, but she had definitely kissed a boy, and she spent the rest of the night helping me catch up on what I'd missed. By the time I took her home, my lips felt raw and my jeans felt so tight I could hardly walk.

"Let's do this again next week," she whispered.

The following Wednesday, I rang Mrs. Quinn's doorbell and she opened the door so quickly I wondered if she'd been watching for me. She frowned at the clouds gathering behind me.

"It's awfully hot out, Dale. Are you sure you want to cut the lawn on a day like this?"

"You're my last one for the day, ma'am." She wore Bermuda shorts and a sleeveless top with white and pink vertical stripes. When she moved, that top moved with her, and I was pretty sure she wasn't wearing anything under it.

"Well, that's lucky, isn't it?" She looked at the mower on the front walk. "When you're done, why don't you come in for a nice cool drink along your money. Sort of a bonus. What do you say?"

"Uh, sure. Thank you."

Over the next hour, the clouds stacked up above me and I worried that I'd get caught in the rain. I cut the outside edges of the yard and swung the mower around in tight curves, going as fast as I could without missing anything. The wind picked up and the leaves on the maples holding the hammock rattled and turned over so I knew rain was on the way. By the time I was finished, sweat rolled down my rib cage and my shirt stuck to my back.

Mrs. Quinn opened the door and her eyes moved up and down my body.

"Oh, my, Dale. You're all sweaty. Come on in my kitchen."

"Thank you, ma'am, but I'd better get going."

"Oh, nonsense. You need to cool off for a few minutes. Let me get you a drink." She turned away, and her shorts were so tight I wondered how she could walk in them. She smiled over her shoulder.

"What would you like, Lemonade, Kool-Aid, water…"

She turned around to face me again, and she'd undone two buttons of her top so I saw two pink mounds peeking through the gap.

"Or maybe you'd like something a little stronger?"

She looked even sexier than the ladies in the magazines down at the drug store, and she was right in front of me. I could smell my own sweat, but there was a soft delicate scent wafting off her, too.

"Did you tell me before that you don't have a girlfriend?"

"Um, yeah—yes—but I do now."

"Really?" She raised her eyebrows and widened her eyes. "How long has that been going on?"

"Uh, a couple of weeks, but—"

"I'll bet she doesn't have the slightest idea what a big strong man like you really needs. Not like I do."

I remembered the drive-in, me and Fran kissing through most of the double feature, even the coming attractions. Mrs. Quinn reached out and ran a fingernail over my cheek, so softly I hardly felt it, but goosebumps popped out all over my body.

"Um, ma'am, I'd better get home. It looks like it's going to rain, and I don't want my stuff to get all wet."

"Oh, I'd love to get your stuff all wet, honey. All work and no play, if you know what I mean…"

"Um, Mrs. Q-Quinn, you're married."

"Oh, Susie-Q, I love you, my Susie-Q." She swayed her hips and looked into my eyes like she was trying to hypnotize me.

"Do you like the way I walk, Dale? Do you like the way I talk?"

Fran's face hovered before me. I felt cold and a little sick. I looked toward the dining room table, where a white envelope lay on a place mat.

"I really have to go, Mrs. Quinn." I reached for the envelope. "Is this my money? OK, thank you. 'Bye."

I scurried out the door and pushed my mower down the driveway. A carpenter's truck turned the corner and headed my way, but I didn't even watch to see if it pulled into the driveway. I hustled the mower the two blocks back home in about three minutes, and the first clap of thunder sounded as I stowed it in the garage. I dashed into the house and took a shower, and by the time I finished, rain was coming down so hard I could barely see the street out my bedroom window.

I lay down on my bed and flicked the volume switch on my radio. I heard a click, but nothing else. I fiddled with the tuner and couldn't get a station anywhere along the dial. I went down to the kitchen and looked in the drawer where we kept batteries. We had some size "D" spares for the two flashlights, but none that would fit my transistor.

The rain was so hard I decided to deposit my money the next day. I'd stop at Broadcast City and get more batteries, too.

The next day was sunny and the lawns were dry enough so I could mow them easily. I filled out my deposit ticket and waited in line to see Fran again. She looked happy without being scary like Mrs. Quinn. I asked her out again and got her phone number so we could talk about what to do. I didn't want to get into a rut with movies all the time, but I wasn't sure what else she might like.

Then I walked another four blocks to Broadcast City. Big television sets and cabinets with radios and record players filled the place, knotty pine on the walls, and soft carpeting like somebody's rec room. I wandered around and admired all the fancy TV sets. RCA, Philco, Zenith. The cheap ones would cost everything I'd saved for the last two months.

"Can I help you?"

Mr. Quinn was several inches taller than me, with a crew cut and broad shoulders. I remembered that he was a soldier in Korea. When he limped, I remembered that he'd been wounded, too.

"Uh, no," I said. "I'm just looking at all the TV sets."

"Got some beauties here." He nodded at an RCA, 21 inches with a wooden cabinet. "This baby is the best you can get. VHF and UHF. We don't even charge extra for installing the antenna. And the rabbit ears make the reception even better."

"Sounds great," I said, "but I don't have enough money. I'm just here for a couple of 'A' batteries for my transistor."

"Oh, we've got those back here." I followed him as he limped back to the cash register.

"You're Mr. Quinn, aren't you?" I dug in my pocket for a dollar bill. "I'm Dale, I cut your grass."

"Oh, right." He put two batteries on the counter. "You live on the next block, don't you?"

"That's right. What are you doing with your house now?"

He frowned. "What do you mean?"

"Well, the carpenter. His truck's been there whenever I'm there, so I figured you're doing some remodeling or something."

He tapped the batteries on the counter a few times. "When was the last time you saw him?"

"Two days ago. I mow your lawn on Wednesday, and he was there then."

"Oh, you do our lawn every Wednesday?"

"Well, every other week. I trim hedges the week in between."

"That's interesting." He put my batteries in a little paper bag and gave me my change. "Wednesday."

"Unless it's raining," I said. "Then I do more lawns the next day."

"That's a good idea."

I felt his eyes on my back when I walked out of the store.

When I talked to Fran on the phone that night, she wanted to go to a dance at the Armory. A local rock 'n' roll band was playing, and we could dance and talk with our friends.

"I don't know how to dance very well," I told her.

"I can teach you," she said. She'd taught me to kiss, so I figured this would be a good lesson, too.

Saturday, the Cavaliers played most of the hits from the radio. Elvis,

Jerry Lee Lewis, Little Richard. They wore madras sports jackets and black slacks and bow ties, and they were so loud the echoes filled the room like pillars. Fran took off her saddle shoes and I took off my penny loafers and we moved out on the floor.

"Feel the drumbeat in your stomach and move to it," she said. "Just watch what I do."

That turned out to be the best idea she'd had yet. When the Cavaliers played their version of "Susie-Q," she took my hand and I forgot everyone else in the room. That girl in glasses looked even sexier than Mrs. Quinn, and I knew the evening was going to get even better before it was over.

That night, we spent a long time saying good night in the car. By the time I walked her up her porch steps, we were both panting, and she put her arms around me when we had a final kiss. She pressed against me and I held her close.

When I got behind the wheel of Mom's car again, I knew what Mrs. Quinn thought I was missing.

The next time I pushed my mower up the Quinn's driveway, there were only two weeks left before college registration. Sure enough, that carpenter's truck stood next to the garage door. When I knocked, Mrs. Quinn came to the door in a bathrobe. Her hair was all messed up, too, not like the neat movie star look I usually saw.

"Oh, Dale." She brushed her hair off her face. "I forgot all about you. I'll put the envelope here on the mat so you don't even have to knock again when you're done, all right?"

"Sure. Thank you."

I started up the mower and moved toward the back yard. I was half finished when another car pulled into the driveway and parked about twenty feet behind the carpenter truck. Mr. Quinn got out and limped toward the back door. He didn't even look at me, and he had his hand in the pocket of his sports jacket. He went inside and closed the door behind him.

My mower was so loud I couldn't hear anything else, but a few minutes later, the carpenter came out the back door and hustled over to his truck. His face was pale and his clothes were all mussed up. He saw Mr. Quinn's car, and when he got into his truck, he pulled over onto the grass and backed down the lawn until he passed it, then eased back onto the gravel and out into the street.

I finished the back and moved to the side yard, maneuvering my mower over the tracks the truck left. Then a police car pulled into the driveway with its lights flashing. Two policemen came over to me and I cut the engine on the mower.

"Did you call us, son? Or was it the lady inside?"

I shook my head. "Not me. I'm just cutting Mrs. Quinn's grass."

They dashed up the steps and knocked. Mrs. Quinn opened the door, still in her bathrobe, and she seemed to be crying. I thought she had a black eye, too. She let the policemen inside and closed the door again.

I kept mowing until an ambulance backed into the driveway. One of the policemen came out while the men from the ambulance pulled a gurney out of the back doors. By then, all the neighbors lined the sidewalk and driveway. Everyone talked at once, but nobody seemed to know any more than I did. Someone noticed Mr. Quinn's car and wondered what he was doing home in the middle of the day.

The men loaded the gurney into the ambulance, with Mr. Quinn on it. Mrs. Quinn stood in the doorway. She still wore her bathrobe, and she was crying harder. A car pulled to the curb. It said "Ojibway Eagle" on the door. All the neighbors crowded closer and I wondered if I'd be able to get the envelope with my money.

The police wouldn't let the reporter in, and they wouldn't let him talk with Mrs. Quinn. They wouldn't let me on the porch either, but I didn't see my envelope, so I went home.

That night, the *Eagle* reported that Mr. Christopher Quinn, a wounded Korean War veteran who ran Broadcast City, came home from work unexpectedly and was acting strangely. He yelled at his wife and threatened her, and then he punched her. She was terrified and got his old service automatic from the nightstand and shot him when he came after her again.

The article didn't say a word about the carpenter. He would have been a witness. My mowing that side of the yard covered up all his truck tracks in the grass. I wondered if Mrs. Quinn even mentioned him.

I saw Mr. Quinn's obituary in the next night's paper, and the funeral announcement. I didn't go to the funeral, though.

I wasn't sure if I should go to Mrs. Quinns' house the next week, but I still needed my money from the week before. I wasn't sure what I should say to Mrs. Quinn, but when she came to the door, she wore Bermuda shorts again and a madras blouse, and she looked even more beautiful than I remembered.

"I'm sorry about what happened, ma'am." Her black eye was almost healed and she shook her head slowly.

"Poor Christopher," she said softly. "He's always been a little strange since he came back. I should have made him see a doctor. Or done *something* about it."

The radio was on again, but it wasn't "Susie-Q."

"You *did* do something about it," I said. "You had that carpenter over every week. And when your husband caught you, you shot him. Then you told the guy to punch you and leave before you called the police. That way, they would believe you when you said your husband attacked you and you killed him in self-defense."

Her black eye looked dark again, and her hands tightened into fists. "I hope you haven't told anyone that story, Dale. People will think you're crazy like my husband and put you away."

"I haven't told anyone," I said. "Not yet anyway."

"Good." She looked at the clippers and the trash can back by the steps. "Is this your last week, trimming my bushes?"

"Yes, ma'am. Registration for college is next week."

Her eyes turned both soft and cold at the same time.

"Well then, when you finish today, why don't you come inside and I can give you a nice going-away bonus."

I knew now what the chances were that she'd be true.

The Cheater
(Bob Kuban and The In Men)
Musicland 1965

The Cheater is a song written by Mike Krenski, and performed by Bob Kuban and the In-Men that was released in October 1965. The band's lead singer Walter Scott received billing on the recording ("Vocal by Walter Scott"), which was produced by Mel Friedman. It features on their 1966 album Look Out for the Cheater.

The School Secretary
and the Cheater

Vicki Erwin

Riding the bus to work ranked among the most demeaning and demoralizing tasks Sharon had ever faced. Her car had turned against her after years of meticulous care and spoiling—she fed it the best gasoline, coddled it with high-performance oil, and sat it on a throne of premium tires. If only Sharon had remembered that a car engine needs a drink of water from time to time. The engine was smoking and coughing when she shared her bottle of Evian. How had it repaid her? By giving a last gasp and refusing to start, no matter what or who tried to coax it back to life. Evidently, elderly Chrysler Neons such as Annabelle Lee couldn't be counted on to live forever.

Adding insult to injury, Sharon had to take *two* buses to Prairie Lea Country Day School, where she worked as the administrative assistant to the headmistress, a fancy title for school secretary. Then, she had to walk a long four blocks uphill from the bus stop to the office. Her sister, Glenda, had suggested this might lead to much-needed weight loss. The only thing she'd lost so far was her good nature. To be honest, she'd lost that within a year of working at the school. Along the way to the office, she had to pass through the student parking lot, which was full of BMWs, Mercedes, Subarus, and Volvos, to reach the admin building. Some days, she wondered if this was payback for her bad attitude, but she never allowed herself to dwell on it for long.

May (only one month more of students) had proven unseasonably warm, making her perspire to the point of body odor after her climb to work. At least it hadn't rained, turning her carefully styled hair into a Brillo pad.

When Sharon finally arrived breathless, hot, and grumpy at the school, a man sat in *her* chair at *her* computer.

Before she opened her mouth to give him what for, the headmistress appeared and placed her hand on the man's shoulder. Ms. Grenier said, "Do you know Mr. Vann? His daughter Ava is a sophomore? Mr. Vann has graciously offered not only to take over as chair of our end-of-school fun fair after the sudden resignation of Mrs. Carter but to donate a spectacular raffle prize—a year's lease on one of the vintage cars from his business that provides luxury vehicles for movies. This car appeared in a Tom Cruise movie." The headmistress sounded giddy as she held up a picture of a vintage silver-blue Thunderbird.

All Sharon heard was "raffle," "lease," and "car." She didn't care what kind of car. Her brain immediately went to work, figuring out how to guarantee she won.

Mr. Vann stood, and the chair rolled backward, almost taking down Headmistress. The man was only slightly taller than Sharon, who considered herself "petite." He had a nice head of hair, dark and wavy, was—how should she put this—portly, and wore rectangle-shaped, rimless glasses. Except for the hair, he reminded her of Benjamin Franklin.

Their eyes met. Sharon felt a spark. She didn't know exactly how she knew, but Mr. Vann was a kindred spirit.

"I shall need an assistant on location," he said, his lips thinning into a reptilian smile. "Would you be interested, dear lady?"

Sharon's breath caught. Would she be interested? Try to stop her from joining forces with this new man and his car, both gifts from the gods as far as she was concerned. She gave him her most brilliant smile, accompanied by a modest nod.

"Send out a notice to all parents about the change in leadership for the fun fair and announce the new raffle prize," Headmistress said.

Sharon and Mr. Vann traded places. She sat at the computer, and he stood across the counter that protected Sharon from students.

"Daa-ad," a whiny voice spoke from the double doors to the office. "I'm going to be late and need to get my books out of your car. It's loo-ocked." She said the last words accusingly as if her father had tried to punish her by locking the car.

Sharon knew Ava well. The first time she'd seen her during registration, she hoped the girl had a good personality—she didn't—because Ava would never make it at PLCDS on her looks. After meeting Dad Vann, she knew exactly where Ava's looks came from. Most parents at the school spent money to ensure their children looked as good as every other child. What was stopping the Vanns?

From the beginning, Ava had complained about everything the school offered, from lunches to teachers to the amount of homework, and even Sharon herself, when she didn't respond to said complaints quickly enough. There was no love lost between the two of them. How could she be the offspring of this perfectly perfect man?

Mr. Vann tossed a set of keys to his daughter, and she missed, giving her father a look that would wither the healthiest of plants.

As Ava left, Mr. Vann shook his head. "I assume you know my daughter?"

Sharon raised her eyebrows and gave a one-sided smile. She'd be politic for now. It had to be hell to live with that child.

"I was wondering if we could create some special raffle tickets and maybe come up with some additional ideas for raffles, perhaps less flashy than a car but as enticing—like dinner with the headmistress or a study session with that lovely Miss Montgomery, the English teacher, or a special workout class with the buff Coach Royal. How about we meet for drinks tonight, around 8, say, at Bar Napoli, and discuss our plans?" Mr. Vann said. "Raise even more money. Make this year a record breaker."

Sharon wanted to say yes in the worst way. The problem was her lack of transportation. She'd be honest with him. Sort of. "Wish I could,"

Sharon said, "but I'm having car issues." She frowned and thrust her lower lip out slightly.

"Car trouble? Heh, heh, heh. No problem at all. I'll drop off the T-Bird, the raffle car, and you can use that. It's advertising for the fun fair. Besides, we can't have our lovely school secretary without transportation."

A loaner? He hadn't mentioned the cost, and Sharon was sure it would be more than she could afford. For heaven's sake, she didn't have funds to fix her car, make a down payment on a new one, or enough to take Uber to the places she needed to go. That's why she had to win the raffle. "I can't let you do that," Sharon said.

"Of course, you can. It will be good advertising for our event. I can charge it as a marketing expense. No cost to you." Mr. Vann shook his head, an adorable curl falling into the middle of his forehead. He looked less toadlike all the time.

She *was* going to be his assistant, and no one had mentioned additional compensation beyond her regular pay. The car would suffice. Sharon agreed, pretending to do it reluctantly.

She spent most of the day searching the internet for information about Mr. Vann. His address was listed in a very exclusive neighborhood. He'd faced some legal problems concerning his stock of cars and their upkeep, or lack of it, resulting in snafus with lessees; no mention of a wife, only the pesky daughter. Nothing dimmed her enthusiasm for getting to know him better.

At the end of the school day, Ava stomped into the office and threw a set of car keys onto the counter. "Dad parked the T-bird in the faculty lot. You aren't faculty. And you're to post a sign behind the windshield announcing it's the raffle prize for the fun fair. As if anyone would expect *you* to drive a vintage Thunderbird."

Ava placed her hands on said counter and leaned so far over that Sharon was sure her feet must be off the floor. "I'm warning you. Stay away from my dad. He's off-limits to other women, especially secretaries." She hummed a few bars of a song that sounded familiar, but Sharon couldn't place.

It took great self-control, but she refused to respond to Ava's threat. There was too much at stake. Assuming she could come up with a surefire way to win the raffle. A year from now, she should have enough money saved to buy a car. "Should" being the operative word.

As Ava stomped out, Sharon held the keys in her fist. So lovely. The keys to escaping her current indenture to Bi-State Transit.

Sharon abandoned her usual care to save game progress (and sometimes documents) and shut down her computer. She rushed to the parking lot to see her new Thunderbird. A group of male students gathered around a perky, silver-blue car that looked like Barbie should be driving it. She compared the license plate number to the key tag. It was hers—for now, hopefully for the next year. She ran her fingers around the porthole window, then shooed the boys away. Her mood changed for the better.

Sharon stroked the cracked seat leather, which could use some work, then slid behind the leather-covered steering wheel. Her palms were slightly damp with excitement. She wiped them on her denim skirt and inhaled deeply. A lemon-shaped deodorizer hung from the rearview mirror, filling the interior with a hint of citrus.

The dashboard presented an array of gauges and controls. Sharon had no idea what most of them meant, but she recognized the speedometer and the gear shift. She stuck the keys in the ignition and turned. The engine coughed and died. She tried again, and again it died. The third time she turned the key, the car purred. Sharon felt power throbbing through the steering wheel. It was exactly what she deserved.

As Sharon shifted into reverse and released the clutch, the car bucked and died. She took a breath, turned the key again, and released the clutch more slowly this time, backing out of the parking spot. Ava stood in her path, glaring and frowning as the car drew closer and closer to her.

Sharon gave a short burst of the horn and stomped on the brakes. They took a moment to engage, and Ava's frown turned to horror as she jumped out of the way of the car. Even Sharon felt a momentary burst of adrenaline as she pumped the brake, not wanting to hit the girl. If something happened to Ava, Mr. Vann would surely cancel their 8 o'clock meeting.

Sharon wasn't used to a stick shift, and the ride home was bumpy as she grew accustomed to the car's vagaries. With a sigh of relief, she pulled the car against the curb in front of her apartment. She turned the key, and the engine continued to chug. She removed the key, pushed in the clutch, wiggled the gear shift, and the car still ran. Finally, it gave a choking gasp, shuddered once, and grew silent. With that last burst, Sharon named the car Dynamite Diva.

Eight o'clock couldn't come soon enough. Sharon called her sister and told her the day's events, exaggerating only slightly Mr. Vann's interest in her. She left early for the bar.

Mr. Vann waved from a corner booth when she entered the darkened room. His first words were, "What do you think about the car?"

What should she say? The car had repeated its failure to turn off at the parking meter in front of the bar. People stopped to stare. She explained what had happened.

"Not an issue at all. The car hasn't been driven in a while. Once you blow out the cobwebs, it will sing like the bird it's named after.

Did thunderbirds sing?

"Can't happen soon enough," Sharon said, feeling her face and the remainder of her body heat when Vann, as he insisted she call him, scooted next to her and put his arm along the back of the banquette. "The brakes are also a bit squishy," she added. She didn't mention how she'd almost wiped out his daughter as a result of those brakes.

"Takes some getting used to, driving a high-powered car like a T-bird." Vann waved to the server, bringing the car conversation to an end.

Sharon ordered a cosmopolitan. It seemed fitting in the cozy, upscale bar. Vann ordered appetizers and outlined his plans for the fun fair.

"How much does this event usually raise?" he asked. "Who knows the amount?"

Sharon named a number that seemed ridiculous to her. The students returned home with some cheap stuffed animals, plastic bracelets, toys that ended up in the trash, and possibly a goldfish that lived for a week. Everything could be purchased at a fraction of the price, yet parents paid and paid until those gewgaws were "won."

"We can easily reach that goal," Vann said. "The question becomes, how do we handle the excess?" He wiggled his eyebrows.

That kindred spirit feeling exploded.

Sharon had her own ideas about excess. Anytime parents paid with cash, something they loved to flash around, part would go in the cash box, and part would go into the special "tip" pocket she'd sewn into her smock. The smock was unattractive, but it was also very handy.

"Does a 50-50 split sound fair?" Vann asked.

Sharon nodded. He'd never know exactly how much she took in. As much as she liked Vann, she enjoyed making sure she was taken care of more.

Ava continually called and texted her dad throughout the conversation. He was much more patient than Sharon wanted him to be. He finally stood and, looking down at the phone, made excuses to leave.

Sharon finished her drink and the rest of the appetizers. Only then did she realize that Vann had forgotten to pay the check. She'd put it on her credit card and charge it against Vann's fun fair take. The fair was a lot of work, and she—they—deserved some rewards.

As fun fair day drew closer, Sharon and Vann did, too. They shared several dinners as they worked out details, primarily those that affected them. Sharon had been right about the two of them being of the same mind. Vann was every bit as diabolical as she was and agreed to everything she suggested. He even came up with a plan for her to win the Thunderbird lease, because, as he put it, "She looked so damn good driving that car."

The first step was for Vann to take charge of the raffle. He suggested she create drums for each drawing: one for the "special" raffle of the Thunderbird lease and smaller ones for the regular prizes: an SAT study session with the English teacher, an exercise class with the gym teacher, dinner with the headmistress, and a computer session with the computer teacher. To keep Sharon as far away as possible from the raffle, to avoid even a hint that it was rigged, Ava sold the tickets each morning, then reluctantly turned the money over to Sharon for "safekeeping."

The idea was to have Ava draw the winning tickets and Vann announce the winners. No matter what number she drew for the Thunderbird lease, he had the winning ticket already in hand. It happened to be one of the several Sharon made a big show of purchasing. Foolproof!

Ava grew more and more hostile. She'd pause in front of the office door with a group of girls and comment loudly on Sharon's choice of clothing. Sharon found her lunch bag empty except for packets of spicy mustard after Ava visited the office in her absence. And Ava made sure Sharon saw her throwing eggs at the Thunderbird, marring its finish. Sharon took Dynamite Diva, DD for short, to the full-service car wash immediately to ensure no permanent damage. The "prank" that made her most uncomfortable was a playlist left in the cassette player of the T-bird (it was truly vintage in every way) that only repeated Bob Kuban's "The Cheater." After that, Ava hummed the song loudly each time she passed the secretary.

Sharon had asked Vann about his wife or lack of wife. Each time, he sighed deeply, said, "Poor Ava," and changed the subject. Poor Ava? Knowing the girl as she did, Sharon did not understand that adjective coupled with her name or what it had to do with his mysterious marital situation.

The day of the fun fair dawned, and the weather was perfect. Sharon had kept a careful accounting of raffle ticket presales. They were already within $250 of last year's total take—and that was taking her and Vann's tips into consideration. By the time Ava drew a "winner," they, meaning Sharon and Vann, should clear a tidy sum. Best of all, Sharon would have transportation for at least a year—transportation that people noticed.

Sharon positioned herself in the information booth—away from the raffle drums and ticket sales—to keep an eye on Ava and the wads of cash coming in.

Ava arrived at the fun fair with an attractive woman, whom Sharon didn't recognize. The woman sat with the girl, and the two of them sold tickets. Each buyer deposited their purchase in the drum of their prize choice. Ava had charge of the money, stuffing it haphazardly into an open cash box. Sharon used that as an excuse to remove bills for safety's sake when they overflowed, hoping the "other" woman would explain who she was and why she was there. But constant customer interruptions made that impossible. Still, the hidden cash pocket in Sharon's smock filled quickly as ticket after ticket sold.

"I'm missing all the fun," Sharon overheard Ava say.

"Of course you are! Darling, go join your friends. I'll cover for you here. Or perhaps you could find your dad and send him over?"

That was not a good idea. The woman was far too attractive to be hanging around with her new … friend.

Ava reached over and hugged the woman. "Thanks, Mom. I'm so glad you came home in time to help out with Dad's and my big project." She spoke loudly and looked over her shoulder at Sharon, a cruel smile on her face as she did so.

Sharon felt a punch in the gut. Mom? Dad? The woman was Vann's, she assumed, ex-wife. But she had never had a concrete answer from him.

The time for the raffle drawing was coming up, and there was a last-minute rush for ticket sales. Sharon joined Ava's mother.

"Hi, there. I don't think we've been introduced," Sharon said as she took the seat next to the woman.

The look the woman gave her made Sharon feel dowdy, especially when she realized that every article of clothing her nemesis wore was designer and perfectly tailored. Not to mention her hair was coifed in a perfect chignon, something Sharon had tried many times and never achieved.

"Courtney Vann, the fun fair chairman's wife …"

That's all Sharon heard. Wife? Vann had a wife? And yet he'd led her to believe … all the nights they'd spent together. Ava's cassette tape made perfect sense. Sharon pasted on a smile.

The president of the parents' association interrupted and made a huge deal of purchasing 100 raffle tickets, then placing them in various drums. It saved Sharon from having to acknowledge Mrs. Vann's status as the wife of her … ex-boyfriend.

Ava returned. "Dad wants the keys to the car. A couple of the men want to make sure everything is right with the engine and stuff," she said to Sharon and held out her hand.

Sharon slowly looked through her purse to find the keys. The car had continued to cough and run after she turned it off, so letting anyone test drive it was a bad idea. This could be part of the reason Vann was enthusiastic about her taking the lease. She wasn't in a position to complain. She handed the keys to Ava, grudgingly.

"Isn't she a darling girl?" Mrs. Vann said as she watched her daughter walk away. "I miss her so much when I have to travel for work. I've been gone almost this entire school year. Fortunately, my mother lives here, why we moved to St. Louis, and she takes good care of her."

Sharon decided silence was the best response to that.

A prick of unease spread through her as Ava walked toward the car. There was no sign of Vann or anyone else near the T-bird. Sharon rose, felt a hand press against her shoulder, and a light touch trail down her neck.

"Hello, darling," Vann said.

Sharon slapped his hand away. She turned in time to see Mrs. Vann kissing him on the cheek.

Vann leaned toward Sharon. "How's it going?" he whispered.

Sharon knew exactly what he wanted to know. She patted her pocket, then felt him slip a hand inside it, and the bulge was gone. Before Sharon could grab it back, Vann slid it into his jacket. "I'll put this in a safe place. All right?" he said.

No, it wasn't all right. To object would cause a scene.

"What is going on over there?" Mrs. Vann pointed to the Thunderbird, which was slowly gaining speed as it approached the parking lot exit. "Since when does Ava know how to drive?"

Sharon gasped. "Ava! Stop!" she shouted, knowing words weren't going to stop her.

Ava swerved to miss a pedestrian, and Sharon could almost feel her pumping the brakes. Before they engaged, the car careened off two Mercedes, a Volvo, and a Jaguar.

Mrs. Vann screamed and ran toward the T-bird with her husband close behind.

Sharon screamed, too. Her beautiful car was a mass of crumpled metal—yet it was still running.

Vann and Mrs. Vann left with Ava in an ambulance in the excitement that followed, but the wrecked T-bird remained, mocking her.

"I think we'd better close it down. We can pull winners for the raffle items and announce them by email," Headmistress Grenier said. She reached under the table and pulled out the cash box, her face wrinkled with concern. "Why is it so light?"

Sharon sank into the chair behind the raffle table, the thought dawning on her that perhaps she and Vann weren't as kindred as she had hoped. She grabbed the cash box and shook it. Empty. She wanted to cry—no man, no money, only a messed-up car. Was it drivable?

Still, she wasn't ready to give up believing in him. "I think Mr. Vann was worried so much cash might tempt someone. I'm sure he put it away for safekeeping." And she'd find out exactly where he'd put it.

Headmistress frowned. "I wish you hadn't allowed that."

Of course, she blamed it on Sharon.

"Mrs. Vann could have taken it," Sharon said.

"No," Headmistress said. "With the accident and all. It must have slipped his mind that he'd removed it." And she relieved Vann of all responsibility.

"Can you do something about that car?" Headmistress pointed to DD as she walked away.

Of course, she'd do something about the car. Drive it to the Vanns' home and confront him about the missing money—and present wife.

The car engine was *still* running when Sharon reached it.

"Needs to go to the dealer," a dad nearby said. "Something's wrong, and you can't trust the average mechanic to work on a beauty like this."

"Right-o," Sharon agreed and slid behind the wheel.

She drove straight to the gated community where Mr. Vann, Ava, and probably Mrs. Vann lived, intending to lie in wait until they returned from the emergency room.

Pulling into the circular drive, Sharon let out a low whistle. She would love to be mistress of this house. The opulence was proof that Vann didn't need the piddly school fair money. He *must* have taken it for safekeeping.

When Sharon tried to turn off the engine, the key wouldn't budge. She left it running. Vann would know what to do. He knew everything about cars.

An older woman answered the door and silently looked Sharon up and down.

"I need to talk to Vann," Sharon said, assuming the woman was a servant. Ooh, she would love to boss around a few servants. And she knew well how to do it from her experience of being bossed.

The woman looked past her. Sharon turned to see what she was looking at. A Mercedes, driven by a blonde woman with perfectly styled hair, aka Mrs. Vann, pulled into the driveway. She parked and helped Ava out of the back seat. Ava spoke, but Sharon couldn't hear her words. However, she felt their eyes burning into her as they stared.

"Mom, help Ava, please," the woman said, then turned to Sharon. "I'm not sure why you're here. Still think you have a chance with my husband?" The laugh that followed contained no joy.

Sharon's stomach fell.

"My mother tried to tell me when he left his first wife for me that once a cheater, always a cheater. And it's true. You don't want to have to live with that. Nor do I."

"It's karma. You should never have broken up that family and left that poor, homely girl motherless," her mother called over her shoulder as she led a none-too-healthy-looking Ava into the house. "You're better off without him."

"At least he moved up in the world when he cheated with me. And Ava isn't motherless. She has me." The current Mrs. Vann must have had something other than water in that bottle she'd sipped from all day at the fair. She slurred her words and hiccuped.

"Leave that gawd awful car in the garage. Vann will be sure to find it there since that's where he'll be living until he finds another place, as far away from here as possible. I'll call you an Uber." Vann's wife pushed past her and slammed the door to the house.

Sharon took a step back. Vann's star dimmed. What else had he lied about? Her newly constructed world slowly crumbled around her.

A cheater? Vann was a cheater. Certainly, if he had a wife and dating her. Anger hit Sharon like lightning. She'd had enough of Vann and his lies.

Sharon stomped back to the car and pulled around to the garage. The door rose automatically as she approached, so she drove inside and parked. The key still refused to move, and the engine continued to run, making occasional choking noises that Sharon figured meant the car would soon run out of gas or turn off by itself. The garage door closed as she exited. She'd best tell someone to check the vehicle to make sure it shut down. It could be dangerous, although Vann deserved anything that happened to him and his car for the way he treated her and all women, evidently. She harbored a glimmer of hope that something bad *would* happen to him.

Sharon beat on the front door to deliver the message, but no one answered. When the Uber pulled up, she collapsed in the back seat, not looking forward to telling her sister what had happened.

She checked her phone repeatedly all evening and into the early morning hours. She tried to call Vann, but the number didn't connect, not even to voicemail. Her chances of getting the extra money and the car moved farther and farther into the distance.

Her phone rang early the following morning when Sharon had finally dozed off. Her heart beat fast and hard as she pulled the phone close to her face to read who was calling. Her hopes fell fast and hard as Headmistress' name appeared on the screen.

"He's dead," the headmistress announced.

Sharon didn't know how to respond. Who was dead? And why would she care?

"Edgar Vann committed suicide. He left that Thunderbird you loved running in his mother-in-law's garage and died of carbon monoxide poisoning. The theory is his marriage was on the rocks, and he couldn't bear it." She lowered her voice. "There were rumors he was cheating on his lovely wife."

Sharon's anger at Vann evaporated, sadness at his death taking its place.

"Do you need me to do something? Send out an email?" Sharon vaguely worried that leaving the defective T-bird running in the garage might be responsible for what had happened to Vann. She'd tried to warn someone to make sure Vann knew. It had to be a terrible accident, she decided. With that, Sharon absolved herself of all guilt. She told herself to be glad to be rid of the cheater.

"I asked, but neither Mrs. Vann nor Ava knew anything about the funfair money. Did he happen to turn it over to you before his unfortunate demise?"

Sharon beat on her pillows with her fist. Vann had betrayed her in so many ways and taken her money, too. "I haven't seen or talked to the man since he got into the ambulance yesterday afternoon." Her sadness shifted to anger over the lost car and money.

"Does no one but me know how to do anything?" Headmistress said before the phone line died.

Sharon knew how to do plenty. Fortunately, dead men told no tales.

* * *

NOTE: In 1966, a St. Louis band, Bob Kuban and the In Men, had a hit with "The Cheater." It appeared on the Billboard Hot 100 list for 12 weeks, peaking at No. 12. The band is part of the One Hit Wonder exhibit at the Rock and Roll Hall of Fame because of this song about infidelity. However, no fictional murder story could be as intriguing as the true story of the band's lead singer's, Walter Scott (real name Walter Notheis, Jr.), murder in 1983. After his success with Bob Kuban, Walter tried for a solo career and failed. He returned to St. Louis and planned to reunite with his old band. He left his home on December 27, 1983, and was never seen alive again. James Williams, a very recent widower due to what was believed to be the death of his wife in a car accident, soon moved in with Walter's wife. When the dead wife's "accident" turned out to be murder, police turned their attention to Williams, not only for her death but for Walter's. They contacted William's son who told them about a cistern on their property that had been covered in spring 1984. Investigators found Walters's body in the cistern in April 1987. He'd been shot. James Williams was convicted of the two murders and died in prison.

The Thunderbird in this story is also based on a true event. A friend bought a vintage T-bird to restore and when he parked it, it wouldn't stop running. He was a good mechanic and fixed it before anyone could die from carbon monoxide poison, thankfully.

96 Tears
? (Question Mark) &
The Mysterians
Released October 29th 1966
on Pa-Go-Go (7-inch)
Reached #1 on the Billboard Hot 100 in the
US, and the RPM 100 in Canada
Over its long and varied history, the recording has been rated
Billboard #5 for the year 1966, and in 2010 it was listed at #213
on the Rolling Stone *500 Greatest Songs of All Time*.

How Many Teardrops

Kaye George

My roommate was tired of it, I could tell. I'd been crying most of the day and night for…I don't know…maybe a week? Five or six days? I couldn't blame her. It felt to me like I'd been crying for a year. My throat was sore, my stomach hurt. It needed to stop. *I* needed to stop.

"Dry your face. We're going out." She grabbed my hand and jerked me to my feet.

"Stop it." I slapped her hand away. But I was standing by then. I looked at the couch cushion behind me. Parking my butt there all this time had put a deep dent in it. Maybe a permanent dent. No, I didn't want to sit there again.

"Okay," I said, wiping my face with a tissue. "Where do you wanna go?" My voice wasn't working very well. It felt rusty. Sounded that way, too.

"Karaoke?" Jayda raised her shoulders and her eyebrows together. Hell, she should know I wouldn't do that. What was she thinking?

I almost sat down again. But I think I hated that couch now. Maybe I would never sit there again. Jayda knew Raven and I had met doing karaoke. Raven, being the one who had just broken my heart. How could Jayda suggest that? My steely glare must have given her the answer.

"Okay, not karaoke. That was dumb. I just thought, you know, back on the horse that threw you."

"I don't think that's how that goes. I think it's a bicycle." She made me smile, though. "I thought you got back on, just like riding a bike."

"No, no, I'm sure it's a horse. Okay then, how about dancing?"

Maybe. Raven hadn't been one for dancing. There would be no chance of running into her at a dance club. One where they didn't do any karaoke.

"Come on, my dear Madison, it'll take your mind off things. It'll be good to get out and to get moving. You're going to turn to stone if you don't ever move."

Jayda was right. I would turn to something. Maybe not stone, maybe a mummy, but what I was doing sure wasn't healthy. Clenching my teeth, I mentally declared my mourning period for our relationship to be over. Raven dumped me. So what? Who needed her? I had a life before I met her at the karaoke bar. And I could have a life now, too. Another life. A new one. Just not in a karaoke bar.

When I came out of the bathroom after washing my face, fluffing my flat hair, and putting on some color, Jayda was at the front door of the apartment, holding my coat. Why couldn't I fall in love with someone like her? Or maybe *with* her? I never had, though. She'd been my best friend for most of my life. She was too much like a sister. I loved her, but couldn't be *in* love with her. I needed to find someone just like Jayda, who was not Jayda. And who was nothing like Raven.

Sometimes I felt a twinge of guilt. I suspected that Jayda's love for me went beyond friendship. More than suspected, if I let myself go there. Like now, when she held my coat and caressed my shoulder as I slipped into it. She quickly looked away. I was glad she never said anything. If she did, we would have to discuss it. I would have to tell her. There was no spark. Damn it. Even if I wanted there to be one.

We went dancing. I was able to drink enough to loosen up. It felt good for a while. For a change.

Moving around was so good. It made me feel almost like a regular human again. Jayda and I danced beside each other, with other people, men and women, joining in occasionally. I think they were attracted to us, the fun couple.

But the DJ quit at ten, or maybe it was eleven. A live band quickly set up and started playing. I looked up at them on the stage. It wasn't karaoke, but it was a stage. The magic evening evaporated.

All I could see, in my mind, was Raven, up on the stage singing, looking down at me. In my vision she was looking down *on* me, with a sneer on her pretty mouth.

I slipped back into reliving our breakup again. Out of the blue, one night, she picked a fight. At least, it felt like it was out of the blue. I don't remember exactly what it was about. Oh yes, I do…I had borrowed a pair of her shoes. Her new high wedges with the straps. It wasn't the first time. In fact, it was the same pair I'd borrowed at least twice before. I loved the sensation of people looking at my shoes. Well, Raven's shoes. She said I'd spilled wine on them. I hadn't. I really hadn't. There was a tiny spot on the white strap, but it might have been there before I put them on.

I guess I shouldn't say it was out of the blue, if I was honest. She'd been acting…different. Distant. I didn't think she was being hostile, or mean, just maybe distracted. I'd tried to ask her if anything was wrong, if there was anything I could do. But she'd shake her head and turn away.

That night, though. We'd never had a fight like that before. She lunged at me, right there in the club. She had just finished a set. The club hired her to do regular karaoke because she was so good, and they figured she would make other people want to do it. That was good for their business because the longer the customers stayed at the place, the more they drank, and the more money the place raked in. In fact, Raven's pay was a percentage of the bar.

So, back to that fight. She came down from the stage and ran at me and shoved me. She actually shoved me.

"Give me my shoes!" she screamed. "Right now!"

was off balance, not expecting that attack. But I wasn't about to go barefoot on that filthy floor. "I'll give them back when we get home." I kept my voice calm and rational. At least, I tried.

She kept screaming and shoving. It seemed like she was trying to knock me down and take them off my feet. Her rage scrunched her face up into that of someone I didn't know.

I ran outside and grabbed one of the cabs that always sat there, ready to take the drunks home. I looked back as we pulled away. Raven stood on the sidewalk, waving her arms and still yelling.

When the cab dropped me home, I paid as quickly as I could and dashed upstairs to our second-floor apartment. I kicked the shoes off right inside the door and locked myself into the bathroom. I was scared. Shaking. I thought I knew Raven, but this was not the person I knew. I had thought we were in love, but that feeling died that day.

I kept obsessing. Who was this person? I knew Raven could get a little nasty when she was high, but this was more than a little. And more than nasty. I was afraid of her, and I'd never been afraid of her before.

I heard her come in. She banged her knuckles on the bathroom door. I had to let her in. We only had one bathroom.

To my relief, she didn't say anything when I opened the door and came out, and didn't try to attack me again. She went to sleep in our bed and I slept on the couch. The next morning, she left early. I knew she'd get to work before the travel agent office where she worked even opened. Probably an hour early. That was fine with me.

I went to work at the insurance office where my own job was, and came home at my regular time. When she got home, late, I had already eaten something in front of the TV. She strutted past me, wearing the offending shoes, looking down at me.

That night, she started packing.

"Moving out?" I asked. "Over a pair of shoes?"

She shrugged, but in an hour or so, around eight pm, she buzzed someone in. I recognized the woman at the door when Raven opened it. I'd seen her tending bar at the club where Raven usually sang.

"Hi," I said. "I'm Madison."

"I know," she answered, not looking at me. "I'm Lisa." She grabbed a box that Raven had packed and headed for the door.

"Can you at least tell me what's going on? Are you moving out?"

No answer. She followed Lisa, the bartender, who had given me a slight nod in answer to my question, and pulled a packed suitcase behind her. When they came up for more things to carry, I pointed out that I would have to tell the landlord to take her off the lease, unless she wanted to keep paying. That stopped her.

"I'll come by Saturday and we can talk to the super."

It was my turn to shrug.

The next day I called Jayda and asked if she wanted to room together. It was serendipity that she had just come to the end of her lease and wanted to move. I had a good location and there were two bedrooms, technically. We had used one for a kind of home office, but Jayda and I used it for a second bedroom for her. The office wasn't really needed now. Raven had had visions of writing a novel and had started one about ten times, but never got beyond the first three chapters.

I returned to the club the next week to see if Raven was okay. I stayed for an hour and that was an hour too long. She would smirk down at me when she was on stage. It was a mean, ugly look for her. She even made a show of kissing the bartender when she finished her stint, long and deep, looking at me sideways with that cruel squint.

That's what made me start crying.

I had kept it together the night she left and while Jayda moved in a week later. We had ordered pizza that first night and watched a funny movie. I thought I might not miss Raven too much. I thought that for a week, until I saw her again. What was wrong with me?

Jayda tried to get through to me while I was on my crying jag. "How long has this been going on? Did you know they were seeing each other?"

I shook my head, not wanting to speak. I wish I had known. Then I might not have been so blindsided.

We came home from the dance outing where I had been traumatized by the band on the stage and the ghost of Raven. The band and the stage were nothing like where she did karaoke. I shook myself mentally.

Hard.

I felt something shift inside me. It was like I changed gears.

I stood in the middle of the room and raised both fists. "I'm done. No more crying." It was like I crossed a finish line.

Jayda hugged me. "Great! Good for you. That was too many teardrops."

"More than ninety-six, right?" My heart lightened when she smiled at my joke. We were both fans of sixties rock.

My cell rang. Raven's number popped up, shocking me. Why was she calling? Then I calmed down. Maybe about meeting with the landlord, which we hadn't done yet. She had kept putting it off, but it was almost time to pay next month's rent.

When I answered it, she spoke before I could say hi. "Bitch." She was whispering. "You're gonna get everything you deserve."

Stunned, I couldn't say anything, couldn't answer her. She broke the connection and I plopped onto the couch.

"Who was that?" Jayda asked.

"Wrong number." Maybe she was drinking. Or high. Or low.

The next day there were two calls.

The first one went like this, as near as I can remember. "Bitch. You'd better watch your back."

The second one was, "Slut, you're messing with the wrong bitch."

Seems we'd traded places. She was the bitch now, not me. But her messages baffled me. Did she think I had done something to her? I had no idea what she thought I had done, how I had messed with her. I hadn't seen her for days.

One call finally told me what was wrong with Raven. "You lied to Lisa. I haven't been seeing anybody else. It's your fault, damn bitch." She hung up before I could protest and didn't answer my call back.

I was the bitch again, but now the calls made sense. They continued, her accusing me and not letting me talk. Something shifted for me. I was not a mean, vindictive person. I never had been. But this had to stop. I was going to make sure of that. I didn't know how yet, but I would figure it out. I couldn't do it nicely. That wouldn't work for this situation.

Jayda had gotten the truth out of me after only a couple of days. She noticed all the calls where I didn't say anything and I finally told her what was happening. I couldn't help but cry just a little when I told her. They were tears of anger, though, not heartbreak.

Jayda came and sat next to me on the couch, leaning against my arm. She felt warm and smelled good. When she started caressing my cheek, I pulled away slightly.

I saw the hurt in her eyes. "Jayda, I'm so sorry. I wish I felt something more for you. But you've been my friend for so long. It feels like we're sisters. Do you know what I mean?"

As she turned away, she sighed. "I guess so. I just hoped… But Raven. These phone calls. What's wrong with her? She left you, not the other way around. Do you have any idea what set her off?"

I shook my head. There was nothing. But she must have perceived something. I needed to find out, and to do that, I had to see what was going on in her life. Had the bartender—what was her name? Lisa?— left Raven already? That wouldn't be my fault.

"I just want you to know that I'd do anything for you," she said.

Way to make me feel guilty. She was awfully good to me and I wasn't repaying her the way she wanted me to. Not at all.

I kept trying to figure out the phone calls. My brain was getting worn out, though. Any spare minute at work, watching TV in the evening, taking a walk with Jayda, my brain was turning everything over, trying to puzzle this out.

A plan occurred to me. I made a few preparations, purchased a few things.

The nasty phone calls had stopped, but I still had to carry out my plan. Had to know.

One evening, Jayda needed to attend a birthday dinner for a workmate and I said I'd get takeout or something. But, instead, I used my stealth purchases, a frizzy wig, a pair of baggy jeans and a huge shirt, and wore a pair of large, black-framed glasses with clear lenses. I donned my disguise and ventured into the club where Lisa worked and where Raven performed.

I took a deep breath and steeled myself before going in. The atmosphere was different. No one was at the karaoke station. A bearded guy was behind the bar. I knew they often used two bartenders and I'd seen him here before. Neither Lisa nor Raven was anywhere in sight. I shuffled up to the bar, trying to appear older than I was, borderline decrepit, for disguise, although I didn't think he knew me. I asked where the other bartender was.

"Lisa? She's in the back, I guess. I wish she'd get out here. We're busy."

"Okay, thanks." I ordered a beer, then when he was busy at the other end of the bar, I slipped around the end of it to the storage room in the back. I reached into my bag, feeling the cold steel of the switchblade I planned to use. Looking back on it, I was out of my mind, but I just wanted to hurt Raven.

I closed the door behind me and adjusted to the darkness. There was an odd smell. Blood? I flicked on the light switch beside the door.

Yes. Blood.

Lisa lay in a wide puddle of it. It had streamed from her neck. Something metal floated near her hand in the dark pool. A bottle with the top broken off lay next to her neck. Someone had beaten me to it. Someone had stabbed her in the neck.

I began to hyperventilate. I had to get out of here. I looked around, starting to panic. There was a door at the other end of the room. Skirting the growing red pool, I made it to the door and stumbled out into the alley.

Leaning against the brick wall, I tried to recover. Had Raven killed Lisa? Had she completely lost her mind?

I had to get out of there. Someone, someone else, would discover her soon and the police would arrive. I ran to the end of the alley and made it to my car, parked a half a block away. In the car, I ripped off the wig and over-sized glasses. With trembling fingers, I started the car, signaled, and pulled away from the curb.

Why had I gone there? At first, I had just wanted to find out if they'd broken up. Or maybe to ask Lisa what was wrong with Raven. Then, going off the rails, I decided to hurt Raven and get rid of Lisa. To show her what real pain was. I had actually had thoughts of harming them both. Now I never wanted to have any contact with Raven again. Maybe we didn't have to see the landlord together to get her off the lease.

When I walked in the door of the apartment, carrying the wig and glasses, Jayda was on the couch. She stared at me.

"What are you doing, Madison? Did you have a masquerade party?"

That would have been a convenient excuse, but I told her no. "I got this disguise so I could go to the bar and see what was going on between Lisa and Raven. I thought maybe they'd broken up. I didn't want anyone to recognize me."

Jayda looked at me sideways. "What did you find out?"

"Nothing. Neither of them were there. Is your party over already?'

"Yeah, it was a dud. I left early."

"I think I'll go read in bed. I'm really tired tonight."

Jayda blew me a kiss. I thought she looked sad, watching me walk to my bedroom. I couldn't look her in the eye and needed to be alone.

Later, I tried to recall the scene. Something was bothering me about what I saw in those few minutes. Lisa, sprawled on the floor, the bottle in her neck. Something shiny on the floor. It looked like it had been in Lisa's fist and dropped out when she died. I knew what it was. I hadn't let myself see it then, but now I did. It was an earring that matched a pair Jayda owned. A friend of her family had brought them back from a trip to Morocco. Why would Jayda's earring be there? That didn't make any sense.

Eventually, when the police called me to come in for questioning, I had to tell Jayda something. I told her that Lisa had been murdered and the police wanted to know if I knew anything about Raven's whereabouts.

When I got there, I realized they didn't know I'd been at the bar. That was a huge weight off. As an acquaintance of Raven, they wanted to know if I knew where she'd been at the time of the murder. I answered as briefly as possible, saying we weren't seeing each other and I didn't know where she'd been there or what she was doing now.

When I got home from the police station, Jayda had left a note that she was out shopping. I had to look in her jewelry box. One of the Moroccan earrings was there. The other was missing. I rushed from her room to throw up.

She got home an hour later, after I had emptied my stomach and flushed a dozen times, then cleared the odor from our place. I told her about the police questioning me.

The news on television that night reported that Raven was being questioned in the death of the bartender she had been formerly involved with. I thought they had been living together, but maybe they had broken up already? I really didn't know what Raven was doing lately. Except that she thought I had wronged her. Maybe she thought I had come between her and Lisa? That was kind of paranoid, but Raven might have slipped back into using again. That had always made her paranoid.

"So," Jayda said, while we watched the report. "Raven killed her."

"But why would they think that?"

"Well, something happened between them, right? They probably broke up. It would have to be Raven who stabbed her, right?"

None of the reports I had heard had mentioned that Lisa had been stabbed. I knew who had killed her. And now I was living with her. Maybe I could love Jayda, after all.

Baby It's You
(Smith)
Dunhill/ABC 1969

This version of the Burt Bacharach (music), Luther Dixon (credited as Barney Williams) and Mack David (lyrics), was taken from the debut album, A Group Called Smith. It was their first and most successful release. The single reached #5 on the *Billboard* Hot 100, and #28 in the year end chart for 1969.

Baby It's You

Judy Penz Sheluk

My Mama always said there's a lid for every pot, it just took some folks longer than others to find their match. Even so, I'd just about given up hope of ever meeting my lid when Mac McCormick walked into my life.

I'd taken to hanging out at the local bookstore on Sundays, sipping overpriced coffee and browsing the clearance bins for brie bakers, biscuit boxes, and other not-to-be-missed bargains. It beat the alternative—brooding about the unfairness of life in my one-bedroom basement apartment, a dank, dreary space that I'd convinced myself was better than living at home. I was thirty, after all, not thirteen. There came a time you had to leave the nest, even if the nest was decidedly more comfortable.

Anyway, I was debating whether a brie baker would be a suitable wedding shower gift for one of my co-workers, and thinking it might be if I could find some fancy crackers at a deep enough discount, when an attractive, thirty-something man ambled up next to me.

"Everything but books in the bookstore, right?" he said, smiling.

It was a good smile, the sort of smile that could win a girl over if she let it, and I found myself smiling back.

"Yeah, you could say that," I said, and mentally smacked myself upside the head. I've never been good at witty retorts. Well, that's not entirely true. I totally rock them ten hours later when I'm lying in bed. At the time, not so much.

But attractive, thirty-something man didn't seem put off, and I found myself blushing at the intensity of his gaze.

He gestured to the paper cup in my hand. "How's your coffee?"

"I could use another." The truth was, I'd barely started it.

He flashed another smile, slightly wider this time, as if suspecting the lie. "Well, then, why don't we grab us a table next door?"

* * *

Martha McCormick was a broad-shouldered, God-fearing woman who never missed a Sunday service. Even so, she'd long ago abandoned talking her husband into joining her. She didn't really mind, though she made a show of kicking up a fuss every now and again. Mac expected no more and no less. It was a game they'd been playing for the past decade, a way to deal with the fact they'd married too young and, despite her generous hips that might suggest otherwise, had yet to be blessed with children. If her eye occasionally wandered to another man in the congregation, the handsome young widower in the third pew, or the visiting son of an elderly neighbor, what of it? It never went beyond simple flirtation, certainly nothing more serious than the women Mac occasionally met at the bookstore and invited for coffee.

After all, such innocent dalliances could keep a marriage alive.

* * *

At first it was just Sunday morning. We'd meet in the bookstore. Check out the bargain bins, make fun of the tchotchkes, find our way to a corner table at the coffee shop next door. There, we'd sip on espresso and share a powdered chocolate croissant, the flaky pastry sticking to our cocoa-covered fingers. But the more we met, the more I was convinced that Mac was my lid.

I was toying with ways to suggest "something more" when Mac approached the possibility of taking our relationship to the next level.

"What's the next level?" I asked, not sure if he meant dinner and a movie or something more R-rated.

"I know a place," he said, and smiled that smile.

* * *

The name of the place was the Sleep & Nap, though it was hard to imagine anyone staying there long enough to nap, let alone sleep. I'll admit to being disappointed. I hadn't expected five-star luxury, but I'd hoped for more than a rent-by-the-hour motel.

"I know it's not much," Mac said, fluffing the pillows on the queen bed, "but…" He looked up, his face flushed.

"But?"

"I've rented this room for a year. Ten months left on the lease." He paused. "I've never brought anyone here before. You have to believe that, Gayle."

I looked around the room. It was surprisingly clean, the décor a step above the usual motel kitsch, as if someone had added a few personal touches. Better artwork. A nice patchwork quilt on the bed. There was even a small desk with a personal computer and a printer.

"Your computer?" I asked. "Your printer?"

He nodded. "I'm an author. Well, an aspiring author, if I'm being completely honest. I suppose that's why I started frequenting the bookstore on Sundays, as if by breathing in the atmosphere… It's just that sometimes ideas get stuck in my head and I can't seem to get them out. But what I've written so far. I think it might actually be good."

I thought about that for a minute. Introducing Mac as "my boyfriend, the author" had a certain cachet. I tried it on, decided I liked it.

"Who else knows about this place?"

"Only you, baby."

Only me. The pot to his lid. I slipped out of my dress, revealing my black lace bra and matching panties. I had a few ideas to get Mac over his writer's block. Provided, of course, he was into erotica.

A girl could dream.

* * *

I was sitting on my Mama's porch, rocking back and forth in her white wicker recliner. It had been six months since that first day at the Sleep & Nap and with the exception of the bookstore and the coffee shop, Mac and I had never been anywhere else. It hadn't mattered in the beginning, mostly because I'd been so sure that he was my lid. But now I wondered if maybe it was loose somehow, like my lid didn't have a snug enough fit, like there was something else I needed to do. Because not going anywhere, well, it just didn't feel right.

"Ah, Gayle honey," my Mama said when I'd finished, her voice soft, the way it got when she was about to tell me something I didn't want to hear. "Seems like you've found yourself a double boiler."

I looked at her, confused.

"A married man, honey."

Married?

That would never do.

* * *

I've never considered myself a beauty, but Martha managed to put the plain in plain-faced. I could almost understand why Mac had felt the need to cheat, though as Mama was only too quick to point out, once a cheater, always a cheater. "Never gonna be true," is how she put it, and I knew in my heart she was right.

The thing that surprised me about Martha, over the days and weeks we got to know one another, was that she never once blamed me for her husband's transgression. I'm not so sure I'd be as forgiving if she were the other woman.

Who am I trying to kid? There's no way I'd be that forgiving. I sighed. Much as I hated to admit it, I'd need to find a replacement lid.

* * *

Mac McCormick considered his options. At this point, he didn't know which one was worse, the bible thumper or the basement dweller. All he knew was that he needed a way out. Who to eliminate first, that was the sticky wicket. Once his book became a bestseller, he would ditch the survivor, find someone younger. Prettier. Richer. Maybe all three.

Gayle had become especially problematic, what with her late night telephone calls, the tearful criminations, the begging not to be left alone.

God, he hated a woman who begged. As for the crying, that just left him cold.

Gayle, then.

Except his wife's life insurance policy made her premature demise very attractive. Of course, Martha's death would need to look like an accident. He'd toyed with the possibilities, dismissing each one in kind. He didn't have the know-how to tamper with her car's brakes, and even if he did, there was no guarantee the outcome would prove fatal. The idea of poisoning her food had merit, but might be traced back to him. Besides, neither of them cooked. They either picked up takeout or ordered in. It wouldn't be fair to pin something on an innocent restauranteur or underpaid delivery driver. He might be contemplating murder, but he wasn't without ethics.

It was a dilemma, no question about it. He'd sleep on it—and *with* them—for a few more days, try to come up with a workable plan. In his experience, rushing these things never paid dividends. It was too bad Martha didn't have a seafood allergy. That had worked nicely with his first wife.

* * *

Mac tumbled out of bed, turned to Gayle, already up and ready to roll, and smiled. He knew it was a good smile, the sort of smile that could win a girl over if she let it.

His smile faltered when he saw the gun in her gloved hand, his wife, Martha, guarding the motel room door.

"What the…" he said.

"We thought we'd help you make up your mind," Gayle said.

"What the…" he said, again.

Gayle shook her head. "Not 'what the,' Mac. More like 'who the.'"

"I don't…" he was sputtering now.

"You never were any good with subtleties, Mac," Martha said. "Leaving that car manual on the kitchen countertop. A sudden interest in poisons, for pity's sake. Not to mention the long-term rental at the Sleep & Nap. Seriously? Could you *be* any more predictable?"

He should have known the motel would be a mistake. It was where he'd taken Martha when he'd stepped out on his first wife. But that had been years ago. Who knew she'd follow him there when she was supposed to be at church?

Martha was still nattering on, the tut-tut implied in her tone. "Maybe if you'd been a bit more careful, things could have turned out differently. That's the bad news. The good news is, Gayle and I took the liberty of making the decision for you."

"The decision?"

"About which one of us should be the first to go."

Mac felt a bead of sweat trickle down the nape of his neck. "That's the good news?"

Martha nodded.

"What's the bad news?"

Gayle cocked the hammer, the pistol in her hand pointed straight at him.

"Baby, it's you."

Mr. Big Stuff
(Jean Knight)
STAX 1971

Mr. Big Stuff is a song by American singer Jean Knight. The song was released in 1971 on the Stax label as a single from Knight's debut album of the same title, and became a big hit in the US, reaching No. 2 on Billboard Hot 100. The song was certified double platinum and was the No. 1 Soul Single of the year.

Mr. Big Stuff

John M. Floyd

"Hello ... Jack?"

"Yeah. Who's this?"

"Thank God. You didn't sound like yourself."

"Bonnie? What I sound like is sleepy. Where *are* you? It's one o'clock in th—"

"I know what time it is. I'm just down the street from you, at the Hilton. I'm using their phone, in the bar."

"The bar?"

"Well, a little room behind the bar. The place is almost empty. You said not to call you on my cell phone."

"But why are you—wait, let me turn the light on. Are you okay?"

"No, I am *not* okay."

"What's wrong?"

"I think I just saw my husband."

"You think—What? What do you mean?"

"I mean I saw him, a few minutes ago. God, I'm shaking like a leaf."

"Well, you can stop shaking. You didn't see him."

"I did, though. I can't believe it, Jack. I walked in and looked right at him. He was sitting alone at a back table."

"There? At the bar?"

"Yes, here!"

"Listen to me, Bonnie. George is dead. He died yesterday. You saw somebody that looked—"

"No. It was him. Big as a house—even the clothes were right. White shirt, no tie, black pants, loafers ... it was George!"

"It wasn't. And for God's sake, keep your voice down. This guy, is he still there?"

"I guess so."

"You don't know?"

"I can't see him, from where I am. The phone's in—not really a room, it's sort of an alcove. And I made sure he didn't see *me*."

"Well, it wouldn't matter if he did, okay? He's not George, and you've had too much to—"

"I haven't had anything to drink."

"Oh, really. Then why are you at the Hilton's bar?"

"I'm here, Jack, because you told me to act natural. Isn't that right? Get out and about for a couple days, you said, let people see you looking normal. Nothing wrong here, folks. Isn't that what you told me?"

"Yes ..."

"Well, that's what I'm doing. My old college roommate called, said she was in town, so I drove over to see her. We've been up in her room, talking, and it got late, and I was on my way home, on my way out to the side parking lot through the hotel's bar—"

"All right, all right, I get it. And you saw a dead man, having a drink. Was he having a drink?"

"No. He was just sitting there with his elbows propped on the table, staring straight ahead, frowning like thunder. Scared me half to death."

"Well, I'm telling you again, he isn't George. If this guy reminds you of him, too bad. If seeing him bothers you, just go out one of the other doors when you leave, and—"

"I need to ask you something, Jack. You listening?"

"I'm listening."

"Here's my question: Are you *sure*?"

"Sure of what?"

"Are you sure you killed him?"

"Dammit, Bonnie, I said lower your voice! And what kind of

question is that? Sweet Jesus. *Yes*, I'm sure."

"Absolutely certain?"

"I'm positive. I hit him with a hammer. Bashed him on the head, hard as I could, as he got out of his car, in your garage. Okay?"

"Yesterday."

"Yes, yesterday afternoon. After you left for the city, for the weekend. Just like we planned."

"You sure you hit him hard enough?"

"Oh yeah. And I gotta tell you, it felt good. Mr. Big Stuff, with all his fancy clothes and his big fine car and all his high-rollin' connections ... he sure didn't look too big layin' there spreadeagled on the floor. I stood over him for probably a minute or two, just staring down at him. We've waited so long for this, you and me. All that planning ..."

"That's not what I'm talking about, Jack. I'm saying, what if he was just unconscious?"

"No. He was dead."

"You checked his pulse?"

"Bonnie, listen to me. He wasn't breathing, all right?"

"I knew it. I *knew* it. You *didn't* check his pulse."

"I didn't have to—he was *dead*. For heaven's sake. Give me some credit."

"Okay, okay. I'm sorry. It's just ... my imagination's going wild."

"Well, calm it down. I told you what happened."

"And after that ..."

"As planned. I cleaned it all up, wiped everything down, took the hammer with me, and loaded him into the trunk."

"And drove his body to the lake? You said you'd throw him in the lake."

"I dumped him in the woods, south of town."

"What? *Why?*"

"Because people fish in that lake, swim in it. Big and tall as he was, someone might've found him. But those woods—*no*body goes there."

"That's not what we planned. You could've told me—"

"How? We weren't supposed to talk for a few days, remember? No texts, no emails, no calls. We shouldn't be talking *now*."

"I know that. But—oh God, I'm worried. I mean, think about it. What if … what if he *wasn't* dead? He probably suspected us already, and now this—what if he woke up, and came looking for us?"

"Bonnie. You're stressed out, I understand that. You saw a man who looked like George. But that is understandable. Except for his size, George was an average-looking guy. And there are lots of big guys in this world."

"Oh boy oh boy. I really don't know about this."

"Tell you what. Let me ask *you* something. Do you love me?"

"Do I what?"

"Simple question: Do you love me? Do you truly love me like you say you do?"

"Of course I love you."

"Then do something for me. Put the phone down and look again."

"What?"

"Ease out of your hidey place and take another look at this guy."

"Why?"

"Just humor me. I bet you a thousand bucks nobody's there anymore."

"Oh, I see. I understand. You're saying nobody was ever there. You're saying I've lost my mind, I'm seeing visions."

"I'm saying you're all worked up, right now. Want to get unstressed? You said you're hiding in an alcove behind the bar, right? Peek around the corner."

"What? You want me to …"

"Stick your head around the corner. Sneak a quick look. It'll take five seconds."

"But—What if he sees me looking?"

"He won't. Just one glance."

"All right, all right. A quick glance. Hold on."

"I'll wait. In fact, I'll count. One … two … three … four …"

"Okay. I did it. I'm back."

"Good. And he's not there, is he."

"No, he's not there."

"See? There's nothing to worry—"

"But he *was* there, before."

"Before you called me, you mean."

"Yes! Before I ducked out of sight and crept in here and called you."

"And how long ago was that?"

"How long ago was what?"

"Since you took your eyes off him. How long?"

"I don't know. Maybe ten minutes?"

"And now he's gone. What can I say, Bonnie? Whoever you saw was not your husband."

"Oh Lord, I'm so confused. This is crazy. I've still got goosebumps."

"What you've got is George on the brain."

"On my mind, you mean. George on my mind. Like the song."

"That was Georgia. Look, Bonnie—"

"This is so weird, Jack. I don't know what's happening. I really thought ... I mean, except for the shirt, this guy looked just like—"

"Well, it wasn't him. Mr. Big Stuff is dead. And whoever it was that you saw is gone now anyway. Right?"

"Yes. Yes, he's gone now."

"And could've been gone for as long as ten minutes. You said so yourself."

"Yeah."

"So, you're safe, either way. Okay?"

"Yeah. Okay. I guess."

"Okay. Go on home and stop thinking about ... Wait. Hold on a second."

"What is it?"

"I don't know. I think—"

"Why are you whispering?"

"I think ... I think maybe somebody's at my door."

"What? In the middle of the night?"

"Maybe not. I'm still half asleep. Maybe I'm imagining things too."

"You saying you heard what? A doorbell?"

"I live in an apartment, Bonnie. I don't have a doorbell. You know that."

"A knock, then? Someone knocked on your door?"

"Not really. Just sounds, in the hallway. Guess we're both nervous. Listen, you mentioned something just now, about a shirt?"

"Yeah, I said he looked just like George, except for that."

"Except for what? Wait ... hell, I heard something out there again. Sorry—go on, I'm listening. What about his shirt?"

"Well, the guy I saw had a big smudge or something on his shirt front, probably some kind of food stain. And you know George, he would never have gone out looking like that."

"See? I told you it wasn't him. Tomorrow you'll look back on this and ... Well, *damn* it. Somebody really *is* outside my door."

"Actually, now that I think about it, maybe it wasn't a food stain. It was sort of brown, and greenish, like—"

"Hey, you out there! What do you want?"

"—grass stains. That's it, it looked like grass stains. And dirt—"

"Hang on, Bonnie. I'm gonna go see who this is. Be right back."

"*Dirt* ... Oh no. Oh my God. Jack, can you hear me? Don't go to the door! *Jack* ... ?"

Romeo's Tune
(Steve Forbert)
Nemperor/CBS Inc. 1979

Romeo's Tune is a song recorded by Steve Forbert, released in 1979 as the lead single from his album Jackrabbit Slim. The song became an international hit during the winter of 1980. *Romeo's Tune* did best in Canada, where it became a top 10 hit. It remains Forbert's only major charting single.

In the Middle of the Day

Linda Kay Hardie

I'm always up for a live show, so when Sandra invited me to see one of my favorite folk-rockers, Steve Forbert—and possibly get to meet him!—I was excited. He's known as a one-hit wonder for "Romeo's Tune," which flew up the charts 21 years ago in 1979, but his fans know him as a hard-working, still-growing, in-the-trenches musician who puts on a great show in intimate venues. He was touring in support of a new live album.

As the midday disk jockey for Reno's adult alternative rock format radio station, my best friend Sandra often got free passes for local concerts. This one was scheduled for a small club downtown on Fourth Street, The Spruce Bruce, on Tuesday night. Sandra was a big fan of Forbert as well, but she didn't look happy today.

"What's wrong?" I asked.

"Nothing, Paul. I'm just tired."

"You're sure everything's okay?"

"It is." Sandra managed a smile.

"Let me hear you say it."

"Everything is okay, Paul." She gave me a real smile.

"All right." I gave her a hug. "I'm really looking forward to this show. Thanks so much! I'll call you later."

I closed the door behind her and leaned against it. I could sense tears behind the smile she wore as a mask. No, it wasn't okay. She should have been as excited as I was. But I would make sure it ended up that way. Even though the only way to do it was to kill Marcel, Sandra's almost-ex-husband, before he killed her. He had put her in the hospital once, which was the catalyst for her moving out and asking for a divorce. He wasn't taking that well, and he was a threat.

Sandra was my best friend, and I loved her like a sister. Closer than that, because I was estranged from my blood family. They never understood when I came out of the closet, never even tried. They were all ultra-conservative Catholics—my parents, my brother and sister, most of the extended family—and being gay was a ticket straight to hell. They never budged an inch on that position. I hadn't talked to any of them in 30 years.

Sandra was my chosen family. "Romeo's Tune" never specifies the exact type of love it's about, simply showing two people who love each other's company. It could have been written about Sandra and me.

I sighed and walked from the front door to my bedroom closet where my gun safe was hidden. I pushed the upper right-hand corner of the towel shelves, and with a click, the shelves swung toward me. They looked plenty deep, but they hid a specially made closet for my weapons. Most people didn't know I was a Vietnam veteran, where I served in intelligence. I came up with the targets for the carpet bombing. It wasn't something I liked to talk about. Sandra was the only one I'd told in decades.

Most of the people I'd told thought I should be ashamed of killing so many people. I felt nothing for the Viet Cong soldiers who died during the bombings following my reconnaissance flights. Nor for the enemies I had to kill face to face.

I didn't feel much of anything during the war. I did my job. I kept my men safe. Except the ones I couldn't. The bombing missions didn't always go without a hitch. Everyone knows about collateral damage. I was responsible for about 400 friendly fire casualties. That was hard to live with, but I got over it.

Then there was the 12-year-old Vietnamese boy who came into the crummy bar just outside Saigon one night selling mangoes, bananas, and dragon fruit. I was a 19-year-old lieutenant, drinking with my men, and I didn't trust the little bastard. One of my grunts started walking toward with boy with a dollar bill in his hand to buy some fruit. I grabbed my .45 and blew the kid's brains out. Chairs screeched as edgy men jumped up. Some pointed their weapons at me. But when they looked in the boy's basket, they spotted the Russian TT-33 pistol he had been reaching for.

I shook myself. Not a good idea to think about the past. That's over with. Finito. I was in Reno now. I looked in my gun cabinet. A .22 caliber rifle. Good for target shooting. Cheaper to shoot than most guns. A .38 Taurus revolver. Fun to shoot. Fit well in my hand. A .32 Beretta Tomcat. Easy to carry. Easy to hide. Not much firepower, but when I hit them between the eyes, they didn't get back up. All legally purchased and registered in recent years. Wouldn't be good to use these to murder someone and hope to get away with it.

Ah. But the Tokarev I took off that kid's body in the bar. A gun no one knew about, from an incident 32 years ago in 1968.

But even with an untraceable gun, how would I get away with murder, without throwing the slightest suspicion on Sandra? Obviously, I needed to kill Marcel while she was working a remote broadcast, live on the airwaves to thousands of listeners, live in person in somebody's busy store, with an unshakable alibi. But I needed one, too, as her friend. So, the Tokarev was out of the question. It lacked subtlety.

My plan wouldn't work if I were in jail for murder because Sandra needed someone to help her find herself again, to reclaim the strong woman she used to be, before she married Marcel.

Sandra and Marcel were divorcing after 18 years of marriage. Sandra finally had enough of Marcel's affairs and gaslighting attempts to get her to believe that his cheating was her fault. That his physical and emotional abuse of her was her fault too. He was not happy with the divorce proceedings and fought Sandra every inch of the way. He didn't like to lose.

Neither did I.

* * *

I pushed the murder idea to the back of my mind, to let my subconscious work on it. In the meantime, I wanted to enjoy the concert. Sandra picked me up from my little house in Sparks that Tuesday evening in late March. She was bubbly, excited about the show. More her usual self.

"I had to go to Tower Records to buy the CD of Steve Forbert's *Jackrabbit Slim*," she said, tapping her purse. "I discovered I only had it on vinyl. Isn't that funny?"

"I'm sure you could have brought that for him to sign."

"Yeah, but this is easier. And I needed it anyway. It's been too long since I've listened to the album. I don't play vinyl as much nowadays."

"He'll probably have CDs for sale after the show," I said.

"Yeah, but maybe not this one with his hit on it. It's been about 20 years."

The Spruce Bruce had a small parking lot in back, and we were early enough to get a spot. Ed, the program director of the radio station and co-owner of the bar, waved at us from behind the bar.

"Sandra." He stepped out to give her a quick hug. "Paul." He shook my hand. "Would you like a beer? First one's on me."

"You bet," I said with a smile. Sandra squeezed my hand. I knew she was proud of that smile. All the time that I'd been trying to help Sandra recover from the damage Marcel had done to her, I recently realized she was trying to help me recover from Vietnam. I was learning to smile. And even mean it, more or less.

Ed walked behind the bar and poured us each a draft and slid orange slices onto the rim of the glasses. It's not a Blue Moon without that orange slice, he always said.

The Spruce Bruce was the most intimate concert venue I've ever been to. The place had original hardwood floors under its classy wooden tables and chairs. There was no actual stage. Ed and his partner Erik simply moved a pair of tables out of the corner across from the door and set up a microphone, chair, and small sound system. I took my beer, drank a gulp, and picked a small table for two right in front.

The bar also had a grill and was known for its great burgers. We were early so I didn't expect service right away, but I underestimated the character of the place. A server showed up as soon as I sat down with my beer. Sandra was still chatting with Ed.

"Will you want to order food?" the waitress asked. Her name tag said Lucia.

I glanced at the short menu standing on the table. "We'll start with the mozzarella sticks and chicken wings, Lucia," I said. "We'll probably order a couple of burgers later, but this is enough for now." I handed her my Visa card. "Don't bring us a bill. My friend will probably want to pay, but she provided the concert tickets, so I want to spring for the food and beer."

Lucia smiled. "I understand." She slid my card into the pocket of her apron.

Sandra joined me at the table with her beer. The appetizers arrived minutes later, and I ordered another Blue Moon. Sandra was still okay. She'd eaten the orange slice and dropped the rind into her beer, where it floated on the foam. Later when Lucia returned to check on us, we ordered cheeseburgers and fries and another beer each. The concert started soon after our dinner dishes were cleared away. I had a fourth beer, with Sandra nursing her second one.

Steve Forbert was playing solo and acoustic. He had stories to introduce most of the songs, and his style ranged from slow, romantic ballads to upbeat folk-rock tunes. He had plenty of repertoire to choose from, with 10 studio albums out, and he remarked on which songs could be found on the live album he was touring for. It was a great show, a full two hours, and Forbert ended with his big hit, "Romeo's Tune."

Afterward, as many people filed out, Forbert set up to sell and autograph CDs at an empty table. Sandra and I got in line, and while we waited, she bounced on her toes like a kid waiting in line to talk to Santa Claus. The line moved slowly, because Forbert chatted with each person. When we reached the front, Sandra went all fangirl and thrust her still shrink wrapped CD at him.

"I bought this just today, because I think I've worn out my *Jackrabbit Slim* vinyl. And I want to buy your live album and the new studio one. All autographed, of course."

"Thank you," he replied. He took her money and signed the inserts for the disks.

Sandra wasn't done gushing. "I've loved your music since the start. I did news at the local rock station in Eugene, up in Oregon, and we played 'Romeo's Tune.' It had just come out, and the program director asked me what I thought of your song, and I told him I loved it, so he put it on the playlist. And I'm a midday deejay here, and I slip your songs in whenever I can. Don't tell Ed."

Forbert broke into a big grin, and he stood up, grasping her right hand in both of his.

"Thank you!" he exclaimed, pumping her hand. "It's people like you who've kept me in business all these years. I really appreciate you."

Sandra blushed and muttered, "Thank you." I don't think her feet touched the ground as I led her out the door and toward the parking lot.

But she was knocked down to earth soon enough. Literally. We didn't notice Marcel waiting by her car until he stepped forward and backhanded her. Sandra fell onto the gravel. I grabbed Marcel by his shirt collar and reared back to punch him in the nose.

"No, Paul!" Sandra cried. "Don't stoop to his level. I'm okay."

I gritted my teeth and swung my arm, but I stopped short and gave his cheek a love pat instead. I let him go, and he scuttled away. He looked like a cockroach to me, even though he's much bigger than I am. Sandra had a cut on her left cheekbone where Marcel's diamond-studded wedding band had caught her.

"We should call the cops and have him arrested for assault. You're bleeding." I pulled out my handkerchief and dabbed at her face.

"No. Please don't. I just want this to be over. My lawyer says we're moving forward. We've got a court date."

Dammit, I thought, this is my fault. I let myself relax and forgot to be aware of dangers around me. That would have gotten me killed in Nam. It would be a long time before I forgave myself, unless I could come up with a plan to stop Marcel for good.

* * *

He called me the next morning on my cell phone. The caller ID showed him at his office, where he's a certified public accountant. I was in my shop. I was ahead on orders so I had time to waste, especially if it could help Sandra.

"What do you want, Marcel?"

"You think you're so smart," he snapped.

"What are you talking about?"

"Stop interfering in my marriage. Stop trying to poison my wife against me."

An idea formed in my mind.

"Look," I said. "I think I can ease your mind. I am not interested in stealing your wife from you. If you'll meet me downtown in the middle of the day, I can show you how you've misunderstood."

I could almost hear the rusty wheels in his mind trying to engage and turn. I'm not a big man. Marcel is taller and heavier than I am. I'm sure he was considering how he could beat me up if we met in person. He didn't know I was a trained boxer, though, and that I'd learned self defense in the army. And later, on the streets, after the war.

"Okay," Marcel said. "12:30. Where?"

"My shop is just a few blocks from the Spruce Bruce, and I was planning to walk there for lunch today. Aren't you just south of downtown Reno? Why don't we meet in the alley next to the bar?"

* * *

I got there 15 minutes early, and Marcel arrived five minutes later. I knew he would come early to try to ambush me. I was standing in plain sight near the Spruce Bruce's dumpster, and he walked up to within six feet of me and stopped, as though we were old-west gunfighters. I had my hands down at my sides, to hide the fact that I was wearing rubber gloves.

"Marcel, you've got to give up and let Sandra go. Agree to the divorce. She sees through you now, through your gaslighting, abuse, and harassment," I said. In my left hand, I held a common Buck hunting knife by the handle with the six-inch blade hidden flat against my wrist.

"Stay away from her. She belongs to me!" Marcel spat out at me.

"Sandra belongs to herself. And I'm going to see that she gets the chance to live her own life."

"You and what army?" Marcel said cleverly.

I lifted the knife and drew it roughly across my right biceps with my left hand (I'm right-handed), leaving a deep, jagged cut that began bleeding profusely.

"What the hell?" Marcel shouted, taking a step back.

I turned the knife around, careful not to smear the blood on the blade, and held it out handle first to Marcel. In a daze, he reflexively took it in his left hand, his dominant hand. I stripped off the rubber gloves and tossed them into the dumpster.

"Aargh!" I screamed. "No, don't! Help me, someone!"

Three men ran around the corner into the mouth of the alley. They saw Marcel standing in front of me, a knife held up, my arm bleeding onto the broken pavement. I started flailing my arms around, as though in a panic, but I was perfectly calm inside. One of my fists connected with Marcel's Adam's apple, hard, and crushed his windpipe. Two men ran up and grabbed Marcel by the arms from behind, just as he collapsed. I saw the third man dialing his phone, calling 911, I assumed, and I pretended to collapse. It wasn't as much of a pretense as I would have liked, but I thought I'd done it right. Fooled them all.

Marcel sagged in the men's grasp, and they lowered him to the dirty ground next to me. Sirens blared as my vision began to fade around the edges. I heard the ripping of cloth as one of the men tore his shirt or my shirt or something to bind my arm. The other man was checking out

Marcel, who had probably already drowned in his own blood.

I swam back into consciousness in the ambulance with an IV in my arm, pumping what was probably saline solution into my arm. "No opiates," I muttered. "Allergic."

"You're going to need stitching," the EMT said. "That's gonna hurt."

"Allergic," I said again.

He put the morphine away. I'm not allergic. Just too many drugs in Nam. Don't want to get on that horse again. And, because we were downtown, we were at the hospital already. The stitches didn't hurt as much as the slicing of the knife through my flesh, which didn't hurt as much as the normal pain in my head, the pain I'd lived with every day for 32 years.

That incident with the kid in the Saigon bar wasn't the nail in my coffin with the army. That came the next night, when I was in a different bar, just as filthy. I was a first looey, military intelligence, former Golden Gloves winner, all of 125 pounds. This colonel I'd never seen before, a large man in a clean and pressed uniform, was drinking top-shelf bourbon and complaining about the troops.

"It's all the fault of these stoner kids," he muttered, looking over at me.

I chugged my beer and motioned for another one, trying to ignore the old fool.

"We coulda won the war by now if it weren't for these boys over here and their drugs," he said clearly.

"Why don't you shut the hell up. We've all heard your opinion," I said into my beer.

He slid off his bar stool, swaying a little.

"Hey, lieutenant, turn around and face me like a man. That's an order!"

I swiveled around on my barstool.

He poked me hard in the chest. I had a temper back then, and that was the last straw. I messed him up, punching him hard in the kisser and his soft belly. He tried to fight me, but I took a step back, out of his reach, and he whiffed. He lost his balance and fell on his face.

The military police hauled me right to the brig. The colonel came in a few hours later, bandages on his ears, a split lip, a black eye, but looking contrite. "I was way out of line. I shouldn't have said what I said."

He offered to help me, but it was too late. The brass had overlooked my biggest flaw because I was doing a good job, but now they were forced to confront it.

I shook my head. I don't usually stroll down memory lane, and it's easy to see why.

"Did you give me something?" I glared at the doctor.

"No opiates," she said. "Just a little diazepam because you seemed rather agitated."

Great. Doctors always tried to calm me down. I couldn't work up much anger right then, not through the drug. Dammit. I needed my anger. What else was there?

"Marcel," I said. "What happened to him? I remember him coming at me with a knife." I looked over at the bandage on my right arm. "He cut me."

"Yes," the doctor said. "You're doing okay. You lost quite bit of blood, but we got you stitched up and we're refilling your tank." She pointed at the bag of blood above my shoulder.

"But Marcel?" I looked around. All I could see were curtains giving us a bit of privacy in this crowded emergency room.

The doctor wouldn't meet my eyes. "Apparently, when you were fighting back, you hit him in just the wrong place. He didn't make it."

How was I supposed to feel here? Bad. A normal person would feel bad about killing someone. I sucked a breath in, but I couldn't muster much emotion. Nothing unusual about that. But didn't I need to show something here? Remember, this was for Sandra's freedom.

"It's okay. Stay calm. That's why I gave you the diazepam," the doctor said. "It's not your fault. The witnesses said they heard you scream and ran into the alley. They saw the other man slash at you with the knife, then you flailed at him with your fists trying to get away, and he fell. Then you collapsed from the blood loss."

I let the breath out. My plan worked. Eyewitnesses were notoriously unreliable, and this worked to my advantage. People usually see what they think they should be seeing.

"Is there anyone we can call for you?" the doctor asked me.

"Marcel's wife, Sandra Garnier."

"What?"

"They're going through a nasty divorce. Sandra and I are good friends," I said. "Besides, she'll need to know about Marcel. They are still married. Were."

The doctor looked at me more closely now. "The police are going to want to talk to you. I told them they could see you once we admit you and get you upstairs."

* * *

Sandra showed up in my hospital room just before the police did. We didn't have time to compare stories, but I didn't want her to sound rehearsed to the police anyway. She had a bruise and a scab where Marcel had slapped her the previous night.

Two officers knocked on the frame of my open door, and I invited them to come in. They introduced themselves as Ramon Estevez and Shemekia Brandt.

"Excuse me for not getting up and shaking hands," I said with a touch of irony. I was literally tied to the bed with IV bags dripping into both arms, along with a pulse-oximeter clipped to my finger and other bells and whistles (metaphorical) to check my other vital signs.

The officers smiled, almost kindly, I thought.

Sandra introduced herself, and the officers nodded at her.

"You've already heard the news?" Brandt asked her.

"About Marcel? Yes."

"How do you feel about his death?" Estevez asked.

"Mostly I feel shocked," Sandra said. "To hear he's suddenly dead in an alley after attacking my friend."

"I understand," Brandt said.

"How close of friends are you?" Estevez said.

Good cop, bad cop? Is that what we were playing?

"Best friends," I replied. "But we're not lovers, if that's what you're asking. I'm gay."

They both wrote that down in their little notebooks. Estevez turned back to Sandra. "Where were you between, say, 11:30 and 1 today? This is just routine."

Sandra smiled. "I was at a remote at the new Rainbow Coffee House on Wells Avenue."

"Did anyone see you there?" he followed up. "What's a remote?"

"It seemed like hundreds of people, but it was at least dozens. And thousands more heard me live on the air on the radio. I was there promoting the opening of the new business. I get a talent fee, and the station gets advertising dollars. The sales associate was there with me at the coffee house, and Ed, our program director, was back at the station, putting me on the air every 10 or 15 minutes. They'll all vouch for me, as will the shop's owner, who was pleased with the turnout."

Brandt nodded. "Were you ever out of their sight?"

Sandra smiled. "It's a coffee house. I went to the bathroom twice. I was gone maybe three minutes each time."

Estevez turned to me. "How did you come to meet Garnier there in that alley today?"

"Marcel called me this morning. Last night he attacked Sandra as we were leaving a concert at the Spruce Bruce. See the cut and bruise on her cheek? He backhanded her without provocation."

They both looked at Sandra and wrote again in their notebooks, then turned back to me.

"I was going to punch him in the nose last night, but Sandra talked sense into me." Always tell the truth whenever possible. It's easier to remember. Didn't Mark Twain say that?

The cops nodded and I continued. "So, when he called me today at my shop, I thought he wanted to apologize. He asked if we could meet later, and I said I was leaving for lunch around noon or 12:30 to walk to the Spruce Bruce. I said we could meet there. I didn't expect him to ambush me in the alley."

"What's your shop?" Brandt asked.

"I sharpen kitchen knives and make artistic handmade knife handles, sometimes on commission, sometimes on a whim."

"Knives?" Estevez said. "Like the one Marcel had?"

"What kind was it?"

"A Buck hunting knife."

"Oh, I don't sell Bucks. You can get those at any gun store or hunting and camping store. Even Walmart carries them. I try to carry distinctive and unique items. You can come look at my invoices and inventory."

"Do you have any idea why he would attack you with a knife?" Brandt asked.

I tried to shrug. It didn't work and it hurt. "That was me shrugging," I said. "No, I don't know. I mean, he thought I was talking Sandra into divorcing him, which I was, because I thought he was dangerous to her. But a knife? I don't know."

"Did he know you work with knives for a living?" Brandt said.

I looked at Sandra. "Did he, do you know?"

"Sure, he did," she replied. "Remember, Paul, how I met you when I bought him that knife with the carved deer antler handle and the painting of a deer on the decorative blade?"

I nodded.

"And did he know you were gay?" Estevez said.

"Sure. I'm not in the closet."

"How did you come to hit him so hard in the throat?" Estevez again.

"Oh my god, is that what happened? He stabbed at me with the Buck and ended up slicing my biceps. I guess I panicked. I remember yelling and seeing some men run into the alley. I was flailing around, trying to keep him from stabbing me or cutting me again, and then I fell. They tell me I lost a lot of blood."

I thought I saw the two officers' shoulders relax. That should have matched with what the witnesses saw.

"Are you right- or left-handed?" Estevez said.

"Right," I replied.

He turned to Sandra. "Your husband?"

"Left."

Estevez looked and Brandt and nodded. "That fits."

"Well, it looks like an accidental death due to self-defense," Brandt said. "We'll take this to our sergeant. It should be routine."

Estevez nodded. Both put their notebooks and pencils into their shirt pockets.

"Thank you, Ms. Garnier, Mr. DuBach," Estevez said. They turned and left.

Sandra walked to the door and looked down the hall. Then she closed the door and came close to me.

"Is that what really happened, Paul?" she said quietly.

"Yes." I looked her in the eyes. "He called me. He was belligerent and abusive. I said we should talk in person. I never would have thought he would attack me."

"I was afraid he was going to do something stupid like this." She broke eye contact. "I'm sorry. I feel like I should have warned you."

"You did. You told me about how abusive he was."

"No. I didn't mention all the times he hit me. He was good at hitting me where no one would notice. Hitting me in the face last night, that was just sloppy."

"I'd give you a hug if I weren't tied to this bed," I said with a feeble attempt at a joke, but it made Sandra smile. "Ah, got you."

An orderly or someone came in to tell me that it was dinnertime. He had a short menu I could choose from, and I picked the grilled salmon with red potatoes and green beans. Is hospital food always this good?

"Can my friend stay?" I asked.

"I can't bring her food, but she can go get something from the cafeteria and eat with you."

Sandra left to do that. The orderly closed my door behind himself when he left.

When I was alone again, I took inventory of myself. My upper arm didn't hurt much. Nor did my elbow, which I'd skinned when I collapsed in the alley. My conscience didn't bother me either.

But the Vietnam stories flowed back into my brain, picking up where they left off, with the colonel. He tried to drop the charges against me, but hitting a superior officer is a major offense, and even more so was my big flaw. Before President Clinton enacted "don't ask, don't tell" in 1993, the military tried hard to root homosexuality out of the service, no matter how little trouble it caused. There were usually people who knew someone's secret, like mine, but they could overlook it if you were doing a good job, which I had been doing until I called attention to myself by punching out the colonel.

I was offered the choice of a less-than-honorable discharge (which was better than a dishonorable one, although only by a little) or a court martial and 20 years at Leavenworth. I took about two-point-five seconds to decide. They brought me my duffle bag and put me on a C-47 within two hours. I was home in no time. No veteran's benefits, but no prison sentence either.

I was on my own when struggling with PTSD, depression, and other post-war mental and physical illnesses, but it's not like that was unusual for me, coming from a family that threw me out onto the street when I came out of the closet. I've been on my own most of my life.

Sandra pushed the door open. "Knock-knock. Are you decent?"

"Never," I said. "But come in anyway."

Her step when she entered the room was much lighter than I'd ever seen it. She was only smiling slightly, but her face glowed with confidence.

I didn't think I would ever feel anything again after my experiences in southeast Asia, but Sandra was changing that. That was both good and bad, I now realized. And despite my family's rejection, I was still enough of a Catholic to feel like I was going to go to hell for what I'd done. But thinking this, I smiled. I'd already been there. Hell couldn't be any worse than Vietnam.

Break My Stride
(Matthew Wilder)
Private I/Epic/CBS Inc. 1983

Break My Stride is a song performed by American recording artist Matthew Wilder. It was released in August 1983 as the lead single from his debut album, *I Don't Speak the Language*, and became a major worldwide hit single for him in late 1983 and spring 1984, reaching number five on the Billboard Hot 100 and number two on the Cash Box Top 100.

Nothin' Gonna

Sandra Murphy

It was colder than a well digger's ass and darker than the devil's soul. I don't know any well diggers on such a personal level I could gauge the degree of chill on his ass, but it's a saying my dad always spouted as soon as the thermometer dropped below freezing. Thirty-two degrees would have been toasty compared to the minus four with the eight degrees lower windchill I was currently enjoying.

Belly down on frozen grass, in the path of a decent downhill breeze, I was sure if my stiff fingers could grasp it, the fog of my icy breath would crumble like frozen cotton candy. Only an idiot would be out on a night like this, yet here I am, which says a lot about me.

It all started as a favor.

Favors can get you killed.

* * *

I met Louise when we were in Mrs. Orlando's third grade class. We bonded over ten cent chocolate milks and a hatred of spinach, whipped potatoes, and mystery meat lunches. Her parents, a high-powered couple who traveled for business, were glad to let Louise stay at our house when they were gone—and sometimes for a day or two extra once they got home.

My mom gave in to the inevitable and converted her sewing room into a bedroom for Louise. She needn't have bothered. Louise always ended up sleeping in my room after multiple shouts from Dad, "Don't make me come up there! Get to sleep, tomorrow's a school day!" We were good for three threats before falling asleep from exhaustion. Grade school is not for the weak.

At the end of the school year, following sixth grade, Louise tearfully said goodbye when her father was transferred to California. We used our allowances and begged for more, all spent on postage and fancy stationery from the dime store, mailing daily letters. We were extraordinary pen pals.

As adults, we became what Louise called boomerang friends—we always returned to each other. I said we were bumper car friends, crashing into each other's lives with good news or bad, then careening off in another direction until we met again.

It was during one of the apart times, I went for my PI license. Mostly, I did white collar investigations, vetting a candidate for a job, credit checks for mortgage companies, background checks for teachers, scout leaders, and church deacons, to avoid possible embarrassment for those in charge of hiring but had no idea where to look for pitfalls.

I longed to be your basic fedora and trench coat kind of detective although I'd skip the hard drinking smoker part. To be ready if called upon, I took classes in surveillance, tracking, and bought the necessary gadgets.

As they say, watch what you wish for. You just might get it.

And boy, did I ever.

* * *

I'd been out here in the cold for the last three nights and two long afternoons, hoping to spot the man and woman who were living, squatting really, in the cabin below my perch. I dressed in camo to blend in and even had an old blanket I'd sewn twigs and dried leaves on. It kept me a degree or two warmer and unless someone had thermal imaging gear, I was undetectable. I wore so many layers of clothes, I looked like a cross between the Michelin Man and Mr. Potato Head.

Turns out, my disguise was pretty much a waste of time. They rarely came outside and when they did, it was just for a few minutes, not on any kind of schedule I could see. Only once did the three of them get in the old beater car and head to town, me trailing along at a distance. They were so oblivious, I could have ridden their back bumper and not been noticed.

He waited in the car, nice and toasty. She pushed a baby stroller, the umbrella fold-up kind and went from the drugstore to the grocery to the convenience store, stopping at the car between each one, fluffing the pink baby blankets in the stroller before heading to her next stop. Unloading the goods, I imagine. In an hour, we were back on the road, destination, the cabin. Well, that was exciting. When it was apparent they were in for the duration, I drove back to town for a decent meal, a real bathroom, and a chance to get warm.

Why is it the old black and white movies, even some of the new programs, show male private eyes sitting in a toasty warm car, sipping coffee, and hoping for a chance to pee before the perp makes an appearance? Not getting that chance is the only discomfort those guys have. For me, there are any number of trees and bushes to lend a bit of privacy when I'd had too much coffee, as long as I was willing to risk the well digger's fate of a cold ass. After all, unlike male detectives, I had to be almost naked to accomplish the same goal. Coffee to stay hydrated and warm, dropping my drawers to freeze my ass off as a direct result. Some days, there's no winning.

As uncomfortable as that was, my biggest hurdles were boredom and becoming one with the frozen ground, fallen pine needles as my only insulation.

When I started this, I had in mind it would only take a couple of days. I was overly optimistic which made me worry I'd done the same when forecasting the expected results.

* * *

It began with a phone call from Louise. I hadn't heard from her in months. During that time, things had fallen apart for her. Roland, her third husband, was found in flagrant nudity with the gardener, a lovely woman who had the ability to persuade puny plants to reach their full growth. Apparently, her methods worked with Roland as well.

Being a Step-Daddy's Girl, Louise's daughter, Trish, took Roland's side, probably just to spite her mom. Louise was able to keep the house, was awarded a nice sum of lifetime alimony, and of course, custody of Trish who chose the most unsuitable guy she could find to be her True Love. Louise didn't stand a chance.

Trish's 'you're not the boss of me' choices left us in her exhaust. As kids, our rebellious natures led us to steal a beer from Louise's house. One taste was all it took for us to know we weren't beer drinkers. Smoking seemed like a cool thing to do—until the first time we inhaled. I think we both turned green but that's speculation. I was so sick, my focus was on not throwing up, not how much we looked like Kermit. Sex? We hadn't gotten past the undershirt or training bra quandary. As rebels, we were boring.

We're making up for it now, which explains why I'm flat on the ground in crunchy vegetation, hoping the tickle on my neck is a stray pine needle and not a spider.

The next day, the pair made another trip into town, same as before, except this time I followed her into the stores. When the druggist looked like he was going to confront her about the nail polish remover and rolls of duct tape she'd tucked in among the blankets, I stepped between them with a question about a fictional rash. I flipped my PI license open for him to see and steered him to another aisle.

I explained the situation and asked him to keep it quiet, just for a few more days. I did the same at the convenience store and the grocery, then headed to the sheriff's office.

Sheriff Bill and I had traded a few war stories, shared coffee and stale cookies, and were now down to the reason for my visit.

"Louise's daughter has always been a pain in the butt for whatever reason. I love Louise better than a sister but Lordy, does that woman have bad taste in men! Trish is from her first marriage." I sighed. There'd been many a time I was tempted to smack Trish a good one, just to get her attention. Lucky for her, that's frowned on now, plus it would upset Louise to no end. "When Roland, husband number three, and Louise were divorced, Trish did everything she could to make it worse, including drugs. She's in rehab now and doing well, but not before she had a baby girl. Louise isn't sure she got a birth certificate or gave the little girl a name. We've been calling her Lulu. It was one of the lowest moments a person could have, I guess, when she traded Lulu for her drug du jour. It took me a while to track who has the kid and where they are. Trish says her 'friend' is babysitting but she's really using Lulu as cover for the cold meds, nail polish remover, and drain cleaner she's stealing."

"We've had a number of complaints about theft lately, the stuff you mentioned, plus fertilizer and boxes of matches. It sounds like somebody's setting themselves up a meth lab. Happen to know where it is?"

"I do."

"Want to share?" His pen hovered over a legal pad, ready to write down my directions.

"I do not. Right now, they're gathering the makings a little at a time to avoid suspicion. They're really bad at that. When the trash piles up outside, they'll be ready to cook. I want to stop them before they get to that stage." I shifted in my chair and then took a drink of lukewarm coffee. "Here's my deal. That's no empty stroller Meth Girl is wheeling around and she's not filling it up with lipsticks and candy. She's been told exactly what to get. Let me get Lulu away from there, then they're all yours."

"We could…"

I interrupted. "You could get the kid killed. Those idiots won't just walk out, hands raised, because you yell at them with a bullhorn. Meth labs are a bomb waiting to go off. It only takes one spark. They start cooking and that baby breathes those fumes, she'll be in a bad way. Let me get her, then you move in, do whatever you want."

He continued to protest and threatened to have me followed. I could see his point, but my reasoning was stronger. "Look, they're not hurting your town until they start to sell. Until then, it's shoplifting. I've promised to cover the losses. If I can pull this off before the cook, we're all good. If after, you've got a dead zone but not a dead baby."

In the end, he gave me three days to accomplish my goal. Baby or no baby, on Day Four, they were coming in like cop coffee, hot and strong.

I spent the night in a motel, had a real shower, a hot meal, a hard mattress, and soft pillow. It was worth a hundred times what I paid for it.

I was headed back to my perch before the sun started its daily climb. The air was turning a pale rose tinged with blue, but it was still dark enough for cover. I stretched out beneath my leafy blanket to scan the area with night vision binoculars.

Without proof, without a reason, without a doubt, I knew he was behind me, on the downwind side. I didn't hear a twig snap, a leaf crunch, or the sound of a frosty breath. I didn't catch a whiff of scent. He was just there. "I guess you wonder what I'm doing here. Dawn is a good time for bird watching. I've seen two warblers, a crow, and one, no idea what kind but it was pretty. What's got you up and moving at this hour?" Friendly first is my motto.

I didn't get an answer, but I didn't hear a gun cocking either, so there was that. "You know, I'm thinking warmer weather might be a better idea than this time of year." Still no answer. What the hell? I decided knowing was better than not knowing. I took a deep breath, said, "My name is Dulcey, what's yours?" as I rolled over.

Staring at me with what I hoped was only curiosity, he was easily the biggest damn dog I'd ever seen.

"Damn, Buster, you like to give me a heart attack. I thought I was about to get eaten up by a wolf. Well, first I thought the guy who's down in the cabin managed to sneak up on me, unlikely considering he's an idiot. I didn't even hear you coming." The dog looked me over. It was unsettling how he wasn't glad to see me like a lot of dogs are. He wasn't hostile like a guard dog either. He was just there.

"So, are you hungry? I've got a spare bacon and egg biscuit." I slid it out of the wrapper and set it in front of Mr. Dog. He had good manners, picked up the top half of the biscuit, chewed slowly, then moved on to the cheese, bacon, and egg, until the thing was gone. He sat next to me and looked down at the cabin like he wanted to see why I was watching so I explained it to him. Like I had anybody else to talk to?

The motel had thoughtfully provided a morning newspaper, full of births, deaths, high school football scores, and my favorite part, the crosswords and jumble puzzles. I had a couple of pencils in the old pickup I drove. Good thing, the ink in a pen would have frozen and left me in a bad mood.

In the afternoon, the activity level picked up. The guy dragged two or three bags of fertilizer up onto the porch. She brought Lulu out and parked her in the dead grass out front. She went inside and he was out of sight. It was my chance.

I was on my hands and knees, ready to run, when Mr. Dog stepped in front of me. I tried to push him out of my way. The phrase an 'immovable object meets an unstoppable force' came to mind, except he was immovable and I sure wasn't unstoppable. His huge head swiveled to look below. The guy had rounded the corner of the cabin, yelled at the woman, and she went to fetch baby girl. I would have been seen, even by those two.

"Good boy, thanks for the save." I patted him on the head and scratched behind his ears. We settled down but didn't have another opportunity.

I've gotta say, he made a great sidekick. Not only was he alert to any sound or smell but he kept me warm at night and made a damn good pillow.

With only two days to go before the Sheriff took over, I was frustrated, worried, and a little crazy. After all, here I sat, out in the woods, with a big ass dog for company and a slim-chance-opportunity to grab the kid and run. I hadn't figured out what to do if the meth heads gave chase. I'm not in the best shape but if I couldn't outrun them, I should go home and watch afternoon talk shows. Then there was the problem of Mr. Dog. I'm not a pet person but I know enough to understand, if you give an animal a name, he's yours. I figured if I addressed him as Mr. Dog, it didn't count. The thing was, I didn't have the heart to leave him behind. I hoped he could run fast enough to keep up. After that, who knows?

It was Day Three when they made their move. Empty bags and boxes littered the porch where they'd pulled out the contents and thrown out the rest. It was time to cook.

Time for me to make my move. I called Sheriff Bill.

No lights, no siren, just a dozen men, armed and ready, but knowing not to shoot for fear of sparking an explosion. Knowing a year-old baby was at risk.

About the same time, I was ready to jump out of my skin, the door opened and the woman, baby on her hip, grabbed a large cardboard box. I was puzzled until she put the baby inside—a makeshift playpen. At least the kid wasn't going to inhale fumes firsthand. Being ten feet from the door wasn't going to be enough though. Time for me to move.

Over the last two days, I'd whispered conversations with the dog and started calling him Walter. He seemed to like it. I told him to wait; I'd be right back. He didn't believe me for a second. This was no potty break, hide behind a bush where he could still see the top of my head. I was going to wander off and obviously, needed protection.

There wasn't time to argue. Who knew what the meth addled brainiacs would do in the next few minutes?

I signaled the closest deputy who passed it along to the others. I began my approach, with a goal of stay at the edge of the woods until I was in direct line with the baby, then run hell bent to grab her up. Hopefully the tingling where my right leg had gone to sleep on me would ease by then so I could sprint out of the way and let the Sheriff take point.

It was another of those 'watch what you wish for' episodes. The first part of the plan was smooth as silk underwear. No twigs snapped, no one came out of the cabin, and despite the tingling pain as blood returned to my leg, it worked fine. What I didn't plan for was Walter being at my side.

Turns out, it was a damn good thing he was.

I'd no more gotten within a dozen feet of the cardboard box when the door opened and the woman, girl really, stepped out. Despite my blend into the trees outfit, I was hard to miss. For a minute, we both just stared. On my part, I hoped she'd think I was a hallucination or an alien from outer space. She didn't yell for help. Made no attempt to get to the baby. Just stared.

That's when I saw why she came outside. And when I knew outside wasn't far enough away, I began to run.

I was able to reach the baby and turn back toward the hill. We hadn't made it far when it happened. Apparently, when you're a smoker, when you gotta have a cigarette, you gotta. I glanced back. Her thumb flicked the lighter and that's all I remember.

* * *

The constant buzzing noise was annoying as hell, not to mention the rhythmic slap on my face. My mouth and throat were as dry as the Sahara, but I managed to croak out, "Knock it off or lose that hand."

"She's coming around."

"About damn time, if you ask me."

"Shut the hell up. Nobody asked you."

"All of you, out of the room. The patient needs her rest."

Patient? What patient? Memories came rushing back, the cigarette, yelling nooo, the explosion and… "The baby, where's the baby?"

That time they understood. "Baby's fine, she's with Louise. In case that bump on the head made you forget, you grabbed her and ran, covered some ground before the flame blew the cabin to smithereens." Sounded like Sheriff Bill's voice but he wasn't in focus.

Smithereens, what a funny word. What the hell is a 'smithereen'? Can I go into a store and ask for a box of them? I began to laugh which turned into a cough—and remembered more. "Where's Walter? Is he okay?"

"Walter?"

"The dog, where's my dog?" Oh Lordie, I just called him *my* dog. There's no turning back from that.

"We didn't know his name. You hit the ground, didn't land on the baby, the dog covered your bodies with his. He's over to the vet's office, got a pretty good puncture wound from a flying piece of debris. Doc Wilson had to operate but says he'll be ready to go home about the same time you are. Also said to tell you, at the dog hospital, they don't make you eat green Jello. I think it was supposed to be a joke but with Doc, it's hard to tell. Dogs find things funnier than people do."

"Okay, that's enough of what you're trying to pass off as humor. Get yourself on outta here, go eat some donuts or something. Nap time for Miss Dulcey."

I tried to say I don't need a nap but fell asleep before I could get the words out.

* * *

Day Four found me at Louise's house, the big one she got in the divorce. It's way too big for a family of three—Louise, her kid, her kid's kid. I think she keeps it out of spite for the ex-husband's extracurricular activities. Spiteful—I like that in a friend.

Walter was here too, torn between making me behave and hovering over the baby. Louise was in charge of explanations as to what happened after I hit the dirt and spent time in la-la land.

"See, meth makes all kinds of toxic fumes so it was a good thing the baby was fussy and got put outside so they could cook. That's what they call making meth, cooking. The fumes are flammable. When she lit her cigarette, boom, the county has two less meth heads. Or is that two fewer? I never remember. Anyway, you grabbed up Lulu, Trish might come up with what she calls a better name, yeah right, thank you so much, and Walter, he saved you both. It's a debt I can never repay. By the way, it's time for you to walk Walter again."

"He just had a walk." I was whining and didn't care. It was part of my rehab, but I'd rather be spoiled.

"I loaded your whaddayacallit thing with music, which means Trish did it. She says it's walking or maybe running music. *Take the Money and Run, Run Run Renee, Walk on the Wild Side,* and one other one, I forget. You can come back after they've all played. Walter, take Dulcey for a walk."

A slobbery leash landed in my lap. "Okay, let's go. Walk, that means go slow. Got it?" If drool equals words, Walter did get it. "We can pick up the pace a little, just don't tell Louise."

Watch what you wish for. Again.

First song up?

Matthew Wilder belted out *Break My Stride,* as in nothin' gonna. Walter took off, stepping to the quick beat of the music. I hustled to keep up.

After all, nothin' gonna.

Rock Me Amadeus
(Falco)
A&M 1986

Rock Me Amadeus is a novelty song recorded by Austrian musician Falco for his third studio album, Falco 3 (1985). The single was made available for physical sale in 1985 in German-speaking Europe, through A&M. *Rock Me Amadeus* was written by Falco along with Dutch music producers Bolland & Bolland. To date, the single is the only German language song to peak at number one on the Billboard Hot 100, which it did on 29 March 1986. It topped the singles charts on both sides of the Atlantic. It was Falco's only number one hit in both the United States and the United Kingdom.

Rock Me Amadeus

Karen Keeley

"Splendid, my boy. Absolutely splendid." Sir Arthur Collingwood was absolutely brimming with praise. "Your mother would be most proud. Yes, most proud, indeed."

"Where is mother?" asked Mark, glancing around.

They stood in the wings of London's Royal Festival Hall, a venerable location nested on the banks of the River Thames, to thunderous applause, the performance an obvious success, the audience demanding more.

Sir Arthur cleared his throat, pulled at the loose skin under his chin. "Stuck in traffic, it appears. An accident at Trafalgar Square, a tour bus collided with a lorry, traffic ground to a standstill. Such a pity she couldn't be here."

An excuse plucked out of thin air, as far as Mark was concerned. His mother, his jailer, the keeper of his miserable existence. She told him what to do, when to do it, how to do it, and now, the culmination of all the thousands of hours spent at the piano in an effort to master Mozart's solo pieces—the sonatas, the fantasias, the rondos, and she couldn't even bother to come. He didn't know whether to laugh or to cry.

"Listen to them, Mark. They're demanding an encore." Sir Arthur swept his hand toward the stage. "Go, give them the Turkish Rondo from Sonata Number 11, such an upbeat lively piece. Then take your well-deserved bow for the third time. You've earned it."

Mark squared his tie, tugged at his blazer, shoved a hand into a pocket, and yes, it was there, his good luck charm given to him by his grandmother. He marched forth toward center stage, a young man, a few weeks shy of his eighteenth birthday, soon to be the talk of the town, and his flippin' mother nowhere to be seen.

At the completion of the concert, Sir Arthur ushered Mark to his dressing room, telling him, as they worked their way through the crowded corridor, they were invited for an extended stay at Lord Grey's estate in Croydon, a delightful setting.

"Grey knew your grandmother years ago, when she too, was a star. Paris loved her, as did Rome and Vienna. She sang like a nightingale." He abruptly brought himself up short.

"My, my—I do go on, don't I? But not tonight! Tonight is your night. Grey, that fine fellow, he's followed your career with the utmost interest, most impressed."

Mark wasn't the least bit interested. He'd simply showed up, done his job, performed like a trained seal, and taken his bow. His mother, however. Where in blazes was she?

There then came the sound of an altercation in the corridor, loud shouts followed by pushing and shoving. Sir Arthur poked his nose out of Mark's dressing room. "My word. He's come. I suppose we must let him in."

"Who's come?" asked Mark as he tossed his blazer on the settee behind him.

"That Robin fellow. Why must he make a scene? Not capital, at all. You won the competition fair and square. He's an amateur, lacks discipline."

"I suppose you best let him enter," said Mark, knowing instinctively Robin was on a mission. Neither his godfather nor Mark could have kept him out if they'd wanted.

"You little weasel," Robin hissed upon entry. "This should have been my night."

"Now, now," soothed Sir Arthur. "I was there. Ten in the competition, each of you given ample opportunity to perform over a three-day period, a jury of five, myself included. Mark won hands down. No pun intended."

"It was rigged," sneered Robin. "You paid off the other jurors to ensure Mark would win, and here he is, flippin' Amadeus, a superstar in front of a packed crowd. What now, you weasel?" He'd turned to Mark, his dark eyes ablaze. "You planning on getting some kind of recording contract for yourself?"

"There's been no talk of that," said Mark, clearly not interested in Robin's bruised feelings nor his alluding to Falco's *Rock Me Amadeus*, a song which was quickly gaining favor amongst his contemporaries much to the chagrin of his music instructor, a tune with its upbeat tempo, the way it captured that funky synth-pop sound.

As for Robin's bruised feelings, he was simply jealous and didn't have the decency to hide it. Mark was more troubled about his mother. Why hadn't she called? Left a message as to her whereabouts even if she had taken to her bed in a childish display of passive-aggressive behavior, a bee in her bonnet. Not like her to miss out on the limelight, fashionably late, or otherwise.

Sir Arthur spoke in an authoritative voice, almost as if he'd read Mark's thoughts. "Where's your parents, young man? You should be with them and not here, disrupting Mark after an exemplary performance."

"Exemplary, my eye," snorted Robin. "If you must know, they're with Lord Grey, something about an invite to stay at his estate in Croydon. Mother has accepted."

"You, too?" Mark made no effort to hide the sarcasm. "The two of us together again under one roof."

He was alluding to the fact they'd been at boarding school together these past three years, forced to share a room, often behaving publicly as combative siblings rather than schoolmates.

"Bloody hell," Robin moaned. "If I'd known you'd be there, I'd've told mother to decline. By the way, where's yours?"

"Missing," Mark told him. He sat on the stool which faced his dressing room mirror. He looked deep into his own eyes. Eyes similar to his mother's. Green, catlike, with just a fleck of brown in the center, long dark lashes, matching brows. What his mother called brooding.

The dressing room was filled with flowers; his many admirers having left their calling card. The overwhelming scent was giving him a headache.

"How can she be missing?" Robin repeated, the fight gone out of him, a hint of concern behind his words.

"Exactly," Mark replied. "How can she be missing."

A woman then arrived carrying a large bouquet of flowers, another arrangement to be added to the dozens already delivered. The arrangement all but covered her face. She entered, pushed herself over by the settee and placed the flowers on the floor. Robin moved Mark's blazer aside and brushed past her, stepping through the doorway to give her room to maneuver. She wasn't in the room but two minutes. Then one of the stewards arrived, him in something of a kerfuffle. Robin's parents were anxious as to his whereabouts.

"Tell them I've gone to the moon," he said, sullen and withdrawn, resembling Mark in looks and manner as he gnawed on one thumbnail as if that would give him sustenance, knowing his ship had sailed. He threw himself on the settee, wondering what could have happened to the great and powerful Hannah Templar. She never let Mark out of her sight, always hovering in the background, even during practice sessions.

Just then, more mayhem in the corridor. A tall gentleman with something of a military bearing, neatly dressed without being ostentatious, entered the room. "Mark Templar, I presume."

Mark stood, nodded, and took a step forward. "Is this with regard to my mother?" He'd retrieved his blazer from the settee and was in the throes of putting it on. He shoved his right hand into his pocket, and exclaimed, "Bloody hell, it's gone!"

"What's gone?" asked Sir Arthur, looking hard at the tall gentleman who'd just entered, trying to make sense of his arrival.

"Grandmother's ring," Mark exclaimed as he frantically patted down each of his pockets. The ring was much more than a trinket of sentimental value. It was priceless, with a colorful history. "I put it in my jacket pocket, for safe keeping."

"You don't mean—"

"I mean exactly that," said Mark. "It's gone."

The tall gentleman offered a flicker of a smile and said nothing, still making no move to identify himself. It was as if listening to what was playing out before him had taken on an element of theatrical overtones meant for his amusement alone.

Sir Arthur had the worried look of a Jack Russel about him. "Your mother kept it in her small traveling case. I had no idea she'd given it to you prior to this evening's performance."

"It was our secret," Mark responded. "What am I to do?"

He lowered himself on the stool once more, leaned forward; his hands dangled between his legs, his thought, perhaps someone in the corridor earlier, Sir Arthur's protective arm around his shoulder, so many jostling for position, the corridor crowded. Had some light-fingered Artful Dodger nicked it?

Sir Arthur took it upon himself to inquire as to who the new arrival was.

"Detective Inspector Nigel Duprey, Serious Crimes, from the Yard," said the man. "It appears my arrival is somewhat fortuitous. I'm in search of your protégés mother."

He'd presented his warrant card as identification and repocketed it with a stealth hand.

Mark replied, "She's missing along with my ring."

The inspector made no comment to that. He turned to Robin. "And you are?" he asked.

Robin told him, explained his parents were in the lobby with Lord Grey.

The inspector remarked to one of his men. "Take this lad. Find his parents. Bring them. We'll continue this discussion at the Savoy."

"But what of the ring?" said Mark.

"Possibly whoever took it has already made off with it," Duprey mused. "Or you've hidden it upon your person. A ruse to confuse the situation. The theft will be investigated."

Mark wouldn't let it go. "It's no ruse. Here, check my pockets."

He frantically pulled the pocket linings from his trousers. No ring.

"You don't understand," he continued. "The ring was gifted to Wolfgang Amadeus Mozart following the premiere showing of the Magic Flute at the Schikaneder's theatre in Vienna just two months before his death. It was to be his final opera. Schikaneder himself gave the ring to Mozart. He built the theatre, a superstar in his own right."

"He's telling the truth," Robin said, cementing his presence as a fountain of knowledge despite having lost the competition. "I too, know the history."

"Perhaps you have the ring," countered Duprey. "Would you be so kind as to empty your pockets."

Robin did, and no ring.

Duprey informed Mark, "Your mother, I'm in need to speak with her."

"As am I," Mark lamented. "She's—"

"Missing," Duprey interjected. "You've made that abundantly clear. But since I seem to be the only one not in the know, tell me more about this ring," he queried.

Sir Arthur made to speak but Mark silenced him with a wave just as Robin departed with the constable in search of his parents, the lad sullen and morose. He dragged his feet as he headed through the doorway.

Mark explained the ring had belonged to countless European royalty over the years, eventually coming into the possession of the Dentice di Frasso family. "They were benefactors to my grandmother. A famous opera star in her day. She sang at all the premiere concert halls in London, Rome, Paris and Vienna."

He scrubbed his scalp, dark curls mussed, eyes wide with concern while informing the inspector his grandmother found refuge with the Count, friends with Benito Mussolini, during the war. The Count hid her identity. Kept her safe. "The ring was a gift to her from him."

"Interesting," said Duprey. "But first, we reconvene back at the Savoy. Larger quarters. More room to maneuver. This dressing room, it's no larger than a cat carry-all."

"You make with the jokes!" shouted Sir Arthur. "Hannah is missing and now the ring. What do you make of that?"

"I put nothing down to coincidence," Duprey replied. "We go, by the rear entrance to avoid the press. No need for their involvement with questions and cameras."

During the drive, Mark sat with his godfather in the backseat of one of the police cars deftly driven by a uniformed constable. The inspector sat next to the driver.

Sir Arthur whispered, "Do you think—"

"If she's fallen off the wagon," Mark whispered in return, "we'll soon find out."

"But why?" asked his godfather. "She was doing so well. Six months off the sauce."

Mark gave a thoughtful nod. "Whatever it was, it happened after we departed the Savoy, expecting her to follow, which apparently she chose not to do."

"Quite," Sir Arthur sighed. "As for the inspector. What do you make of him?"

Mark shrugged without comment.

The day's cloud cover threatened rain, night having fallen, just gone 10 o'clock. London resembled the look of Gustave Caillebotte's painting, Paris Street; Rainy Day, a city transformed.

An ambulance sped past, siren blaring, lights flashing, the vehicle headed in the opposite direction. The rhythmic tone of the windshield wipers, almost hypnotic, added to Mark's turmoil. Would his mother tear a strip off him when she found out the ring was missing? And what of Sir Arthur? He looked a man filled with impending doom; his head headed for the chopping block through negligence. When it came to Mark, Hannah Templar expected Sir Arthur to guard her son with his life. The lad and his property.

When they arrived at the Savoy near London's West End, Mark led the way. He and his mother shared an interconnecting suite, their rooms too, overlooking the River Thames, the hotel known for its theatrical flair.

Upon entry, the inspector said, "This is your shared suite?"

"Yes, but what's happened?" The suite was in disarray, a lamp overturned, Mark's mother's jewelry case emptied of its contents, and no sign of her.

"We were led to a different room earlier," Duprey replied. "An obvious mix-up."

He took a turn around the suite, those in attendance with him, all congregated at the door.

Falco's *Rock Me Amadeus* played on Mark's radio/cassette player in his section of the suite. He went through a doorway to his left and turned off the cassette, formerly rigged to play in a loop. When he returned, he stated, "You mentioned serious crimes. Are you accusing my mother of some indiscretion?"

"Not at all," replied the inspector. "But the Dentice di Frasso family have come forward and alleged the ring you referenced was stolen during the war, 18K gold and inscribed with the Thun-Hohenstein family crest, Mozart's staunchest supporters, I was told. The family want the ring returned."

"But it was gifted to my grandmother," said Mark. "Then to me. And why now? It's forty years since the war."

"My task is to speak with your mother. I find it intriguing the ring goes missing this night."

What the inspector had yet to learn, his mother, not fond of children, had simply done her duty, his father absent much of the time due to his business interests. If not for Sir Arthur Collingwood, Mark's godfather, a longtime family friend, Mark wouldn't have had a male role model in his life but for the teachers at his boarding school.

Now, at age eighteen, music was changing yet again. No more Motown, psychedelic rock, or the British Invasion. It was Wham!, Madonna and Dire Straits. When Falco's *Rock Me Amadeus* proved to be a big hit, especially in Europe, he and Robin were deemed the Amadeus twins. "I suppose this means I'm Salieri to your Mozart," Robin acquiesced, both lads having heard the story, a perceived feud between two talented composers, never proven, but the allegation persisted. On those nights, in the privacy of their dorm room, gloves off, they'd listened to Falco's song, each wanting to be a superstar.

On the credenza near Mark's bed was a photograph of Mark and his mother, a woman with a formidable presence; high cheekbones, sensuous lips, and dark raven hair.

"Your mother, I presume." Duprey gave the photograph a disparaging look, a woman not to be trifled with while noting Mark's resemblance which proved the apple didn't fall far from the tree.

Mark nodded. "I don't understand. Has someone abducted her? Could she be held for ransom?"

"Let's not get ahead of ourselves," said the inspector. "All of you. Come. Find seating. The chairs, the settee. We're going to have a discussion."

They did as Duprey requested.

Obviously worried, Mark told the inspector, "You don't know her. One moment, she's weeping with rage because I played a C-flat minor inversion when it's well-known Mozart used no such combination in his compositions. The next, she's singing my praises, a genius in my own right. My life has been a series of ups and downs, riding an emotional rollercoaster, never knowing which comes next, praise or reproach, but she is—she was my mother."

"You speak as if you have knowledge as to her whereabouts, possibly with an untidy ending."

"Untidy," murmured Mark. "Yes, I suppose you could put it that way."

Sir Arthur then spoke, "Hannah is a woman with a most temperamental nature, even as a child, spoiled for much of her life. She grew into an overbearing demanding woman, but none of us present would have wished her harm."

"I've made no such accusation," said Duprey. "And you, Mark's godfather."

Sir Arthur bristled, the cheek of the man implying improprieties in that regard.

"That was due to Mark's grandmother, she too, a formidable woman with a stage presence. Our families owned property in Essex near Colchester. We were precocious children in spirit and manner, often finding folly in the most unlikely of places which greatly upset our elders. This at a time children were meant to be seen and not heard, paraded about the countryside in order to meet the right people, expected to behave with dignity and decorum."

Of that, I have no doubt, thought Duprey. England and its social classes, and never the twain shall meet, but alas, the hierarchy of one's station in life led to many a crime which needed solving, the haves versus the have-nots.

"And what of Mark's grandmother. Is she still alive?"

Sir Arthur shook his head. "She died some three years ago. Mark's mother, Hannah, saw little of her growing up, handed off to nannies and governesses. The two women were not close."

It was then; Mark's defenses broke down, all this talk of his grandmother, she the only one to have shown him any true affection. The conversation took a sharp ninety-degree turn. He told Duprey, "Robin and me, the snide remarks, the arguing, it's nothing more than pretense."

The inspector nodded thoughtfully. "You're more than schoolmates, you mean?"

Mark nodded, said no more. What was unspoken was now the elephant in the room.

"What's that?" sputtered Robin's father. "My son? Never!"

"It's been known to happen, Mr. Glover." Duprey knew from personal experience, the heart wants what the heart wants, but he kept those thoughts to himself. It might be the eighties, but for many, the stigma of being ostracized still reared its ugly head.

"Who knew?" he asked the boys.

"Mother found out," said Mark. "She discovered some poems. Thought they were to a girl. When she realized their true nature, she became angry, told me, if word got out, the scandal would ruin my career before it's even begun. Reception then telephoned to say Sir Arthur had arrived. Mother told me to go, to get out of her sight. I left her here, and met Sir Arthur downstairs in the main lobby."

Sir Arthur nodded, corroborating that bit of information.

"And between the time you departed, and the start of the concert, you were together?"

Again, Sir Arthur nodded. He looked intently at Mark, then at Robin, as if he'd only just now seen both boys for who they really were. Young men, on the brink of discovery, a changing world in oh, so many ways. Not just the music. But still, Sir Arthur's generation, old school. Best to let sleeping dogs lie.

Mark continued, "When Robin and I developed feelings for each other, we knew we had to keep it secret. And what better way than to escalate the rivalry. We've competed in most everything—sports, academics, the music. If word got out, we'd have been teased and taunted at school, bullied even. And our parents! They'd have seen it as a character assassination against themselves. My mother made that abundantly clear."

Mark looked at Robin with such tenderness, Robin felt as if he'd cry.

"All of it's true," he said. "What Mark is telling you."

Robin's mother, sitting like a statue, confirmed Mark's hypothesis. Her face stated for all and sundry, she'd spawned Satan's child. Robin snorted, "Look at them, inspector! I'm still me, mother. Nothing has changed."

The woman shivered, stiffened her spine, and displayed the quintessential English stiff upper lip. Robin knew she'd be thinking, this was not the time nor the place to make a public scene. "We'll speak of this later," she said, her tone implying Mark's words were insufferable, meant to disparage her own son's reputation, nothing but lies.

"And the ring?" asked Duprey.

"If you must know," said Robin, "I took it from Mark's blazer pocket. I knew he'd have it hidden there. It was his lucky charm despite how his mother felt about it, the ring gifted to Mark and not to her. I gave it to the person who delivered the flowers."

"What flowers?" remarked the inspector.

"Just before your arrival," said Sir Arthur. "A large bouquet delivered."

"I didn't see a face," Mark replied. "I've no idea who it was."

Robin sighed, folded his hands and stared at his thumbs. "It was my sister pretending to work for the hall. She wanted to see the dressing room, to give Mark a dressing down. She believed I'd been cheated out of the win. She was angry. I pretended to be. The gist of it was, I was proud of Mark but I couldn't let Emily know that. I gave her the ring. She knew how much it meant to Mark and she wanted to give him a fright. She wouldn't have kept it. My sister is not a thief."

Duprey turned to the Glovers. "Where's your daughter now?"

"She'd be at home," said Robin's father, his mind still reeling, he too, navigating the invisible elephant in the room.

Duprey spoke with his sergeant. During their quiet *tête-à-tête*, Mark figured he was probably telling his subordinate to ensure Emily had the ring and to bring it, and the girl, to the Savoy. The cat out of the bag, as it were. It surprised him Emily had done such a thing. But he also knew, she was hurt, believing her fraternal twin cheated out of his chance at stardom.

"Is that necessary?" asked Sir Arthur. "Surely you could go yourself, speak with the child, retrieve the ring. You need not escalate the situation, no harm done."

"I could, but as you can see, I'm quite tied up here."

He then asked Mark, why classical music, why the interest?

Why the silly question? What did that have to do with anything? Rather than argue, he told Duprey, "My grandmother was fond of Mozart, her favorite composer. At age fourteen, he decided to call himself Amadé because he liked the sound of it. By the time he was in his twenties, he'd become a free mason, the secret society known for its charitable works. I think, for Mozart, it was a way to belong. Something outside of his music. He needed the companionship of other men, likeminded men, and he found them."

"Meaning?" asked Duprey.

"It was no different for Robin and me. We had our secret handshake, our rituals."

"Such as?"

"Ours to know, yours to find out. Not pertinent to your investigation."

If he was now coming across as belligerent, so be it. He was angry. He had every right to be angry. Whether he loved his mother, or not, she was his mother, the woman who bore him, gave him life, and this infuriating inspector asking ridiculous questions.

"Everything is pertinent during an investigation," Duprey said. "Until we rule it out."

Robin interjected. "A silver medallion," he said. "You might as well tell him, Mark. We each have one, Remus and Romulus. Twins, metaphorically abandoned as infants and nursed by she-wolves, the story of our lives. One founded the city of Rome, according to myth. We keep it here," he pulled at his tie, loosened it, that and his shirt collar, and produced a silver chain about his neck.

Robin's mother had obviously taken exception to his metaphor; the implication she was a she-wolf. If looks could have turned her son into a pillar of salt, she'd have won that round.

Duprey asked Mark, "And yours?"

"I didn't wear it tonight. It's in the bureau. Mother must have found it, another something to make her angry."

"What do you think has happened to her?"

"As I've told you, given the state of the room, the lamp toppled, her jewelry case empty, she was abducted. You're wasting time debating absurd details which have nothing to do with her disappearance."

A compatriot of Duprey's entered the room, motioned for a word. They spoke but a few sentences and Duprey turned to the group. "A woman's body has been discovered, a suspicious death. It could be Hannah Templar."

Mark jumped to his feet, grabbed his godfather's right arm. Sir Arthur stood somewhat wobbly given the shock of the news. Robin and his parents sat, dumbstruck.

"You're all to remain here, with this officer. I'll return as quickly as I can."

Quickly became two hours, which dragged by, everyone's nerves as taught as piano wire.

During Duprey's absence, Emily arrived, brought to the hotel by another constable. She ran to her parents, threw herself into their arms and burst into tears. "I didn't mean anything by it," she cried. "I wanted Mark to suffer, just as Robin has suffered. Here—here's the ruddy thing and I hope Mark chokes on it!"

She threw the ring at Mark. He caught it, processing the ire in Emily's red-rimmed eyes, plenty of tears during the drive to the hotel, complicit in the theft of the ring. He held no ill will toward Robin nor

Emily. She however, was full of questions, of which her parents provided the answers as best they could.

When the inspector returned, he confirmed the deceased was that of Hannah Templar who'd been found dead in an alley behind the concert hall. "It's proving difficult to establish time of death given the change in weather. I need each of you to tell me where you were, who you were with, and what you were doing from six o'clock on."

Dead? His mother dead? Mark couldn't believe it. And this Duprey fellow acting as if he'd just rattled off the race results at Ascot Racecourse with all the Royals in attendance.

"But how?" he finally managed to blurt out.

"Blunt force trauma to the head," said the inspector. "Her body had been dragged farther down the alley, half hidden behind a large commercial dust bin."

"Who found her?" asked Robin.

"All in due course. I understand everyone's in shock, your disbelief." He addressed Mark directly. "I extend my condolences to you. And to Sir Arthur."

"Thank you," said Sir Arthur, more by rote than any genuine feeling of gratitude. Hannah had been a force of nature, and many an argument he'd had with her, but he'd never have wished her dead.

"She did come," breathed Mark, more to himself than anyone else. "She wasn't drinking. No one abducted her. She must have emptied the jewelry case herself, bumped the lamp in her haste to leave the room."

"A sensible deduction," observed the inspector.

"Stands to reason, doesn't it? If she was found near the hall, she came."

"Or was forced there," countered Duprey. "We have questions that need answers, and I mean to have them."

He led the investigation through several lines of inquiry, eventually getting closer to the truth. He turned his gaze to Emily. She sat sandwiched between her parents, all three on the settee. She appeared older than her brother despite the two of them being twins, both fair-haired with a spattering of freckles across their noses, possibly because of the lipstick, her chic hairstyle, her designer outfit most likely purchased in Bond Street at one of the high-end boutiques.

She gave Duprey a defiant look, a definite challenge. "It came down to blackmail, didn't it, young lady?" He stood with his thumbs in the pockets of his waistcoat looking somewhat cavalier, ready to pounce.

"Why would you think that?" she said.

"I say, inspector. What the devil are you playing at?" George Glover had raised his voice, a man in desperate need to protect his daughter, unsure of what to do next.

The inspector continued, "You discovered the true nature of your brother's relationship with Mark. That only intensified your desire to destroy Mark's career. To do that, you needed to tarnish his name. That's where the blackmail came in."

Emily snorted. "You're speaking nonsense."

"You stole the ring."

"If you say so. Robin gave it to me."

"Only because you threatened him."

"You can't possibly know that."

"Oh, but I do. My sergeant spoke with one of the housemaids. You were overheard speaking with Hannah Templar on the upstairs telephone. You knew Mark and Robin were more than roommates. You threatened exposure, to your parents to be precise, and wouldn't that have upset the applecart, their fair-haired boy not at all the son they thought he was."

"I did no such thing," Emily sneered. "I wanted Mark to suffer for having won the competition."

Duprey parted the drapes and peered into the night, knowing many a perpetrator had wanted their victim to suffer. "You told Hannah Templar to bring money. And if not money, then jewels, whatever she had, to the hall. Only then would you not go to the tabloids and reveal what you knew about your brother and Mark Templar."

Robin spoke up, his voice cracked with emotion. "Em, what did you do?"

"I didn't do anything," she said. "The inspector is grabbing at straws. The next thing we know, he'll be accusing you, then mother, then father. Even that deplorable man," and she pointed at Sir Arthur. "It's all his fault for having rigged the competition."

"I say," sputtered Sir Arthur. "I did no such thing!"

"But you did," Emily shouted. "Robin told me."

"I lied," said Robin. "I didn't think you'd act on it, that you'd seek out some kind of revenge. When you said you wanted the ring, I admit, I went along with it in order to keep up the ruse between Mark and me, the rivalry. But murder? How could you?"

The fight then left Emily. "I did it for you, dear brother. Each of you vying to be best, and for what! You were the best. Until that man," she again pointed to Sir Arthur, "ruined it. You told me, he and Mark's mother bribed the other jurors in Mark's favor; you were cheated out of the competition."

"Mark won fair 'n square," Robin lamented. "No one cheated."

"But you said—"

"I should have said nothing, Em. It's all my fault." Robin was fighting to hold back the tears. "I'm sorry."

"Sorry?" exclaimed his sister. "A bit late for that, wouldn't you say? And her death was an accident. She made me so angry, so very *very* angry. She laughed when she realized who I was, treated me as if I were some insolent child in the throes of a tantrum. She stood there with her holier than thou attitude, alluding to the fact her dear boy was the second Messiah given his God-given talent, that Mark had been a child prodigy just like Mozart, playing the keyboard and violin by age five, writing his own compositions. That you, Robin, had no talent. Not like Mark, and you do have talent. I've heard you play; you play beautifully."

"Oh, my dear girl," her mother cried. "You've destroyed your future."

"What future? Marriage, children? I want none of that. I wanted to travel, to become a photojournalist, but no. You wouldn't support my dream. But Robin, nothing too good for him."

"You did it out of spite, out of jealousy?" asked her mother.

"No," said Emily. She paused for effect, all eyes on her, the spotlight taken off that damnable Mark Templar, she now the center of attention. "If you must know, I did it for love. For Robin. I never begrudged him his success. It wasn't his fault you doted on him hand and foot, spoiling him. But even so, if my dream couldn't come true, perhaps his could. Whether money or jewels, I'd have given it back. I simply wanted to frighten her. To make her feel the pain, the humiliation, Robin felt, losing the competition. I truly believed it had been rigged, Sir Arthur and that appalling Hannah Templar jointly involved. I grabbed a piece of rebar discarded in the alley. I don't remember using it, but there you have it."

She turned to the inspector. "Will you now arrest me?" She appeared quite calm, totally in control.

"Time to face the music," said Detective Inspector Nigel Duprey. He cautioned her while her parents and her brother looked on, unable to do anything to help her.

All Mark could think—rock me, Amadeus—his world rocked right off its axis. The fact his godfather had praised his performance following the concert meant nothing. He did not feel like a superstar. He had no flair. He'd never been popular. He'd never been to Vienna.

Sir Arthur stood in the shadows. "Yes indeed," he muttered. "Time to face the music." Secrets, assumptions and innuendo, and look where it led? Lives destroyed, Hannah murdered, Robin's sister most likely headed to prison, and for what?

He then wondered if the Dentice di Frasso family had somehow become suspicious of his and Lord Grey's covert business practices during the war, much of it taking place incognito behind the Count's back despite their combined friendship with Benito Mussolini. It was well known religious artifacts and priceless artwork were stolen and smuggled out of Italy, many of the items sold on the black market. Maybe the real reason the family believed the ring was stolen, the reason for the inspector's involvement, he too, taking up a shovel so that he could begin his own archeological excavation into affairs long past. No matter, thought Sir Arthur. He knew the ring to be a legitimate gift. Proving it could be a whole other kettle of fish.

In the meantime, best to come clean. He would inform his godson, his mother was the illegitimate daughter to Lord Grey, sixth Viscount of Croydon, something she herself never knew, following a short but passionate *affare illecito* with Mark's grandmother.

Grey's marriage as a devout Catholic meant he could not lay claim to Mark as his legitimate grandson who now stood on the brink of greatness, destined to become something of a superstar in his own right. He could however, offer the lad sanctuary away from the press and paparazzi, time enough to heal from the unfortunate death of his mother. And rightly so.

Excellence flowed through Mark's veins just as it had with the great Maria Von Droste zu Hülshoff. And who better to take on the roll as business manager than Grey? Sir Arthur was well acquainted with Grey's business acumen, theirs a long and sordid history. Serious crimes, indeed!

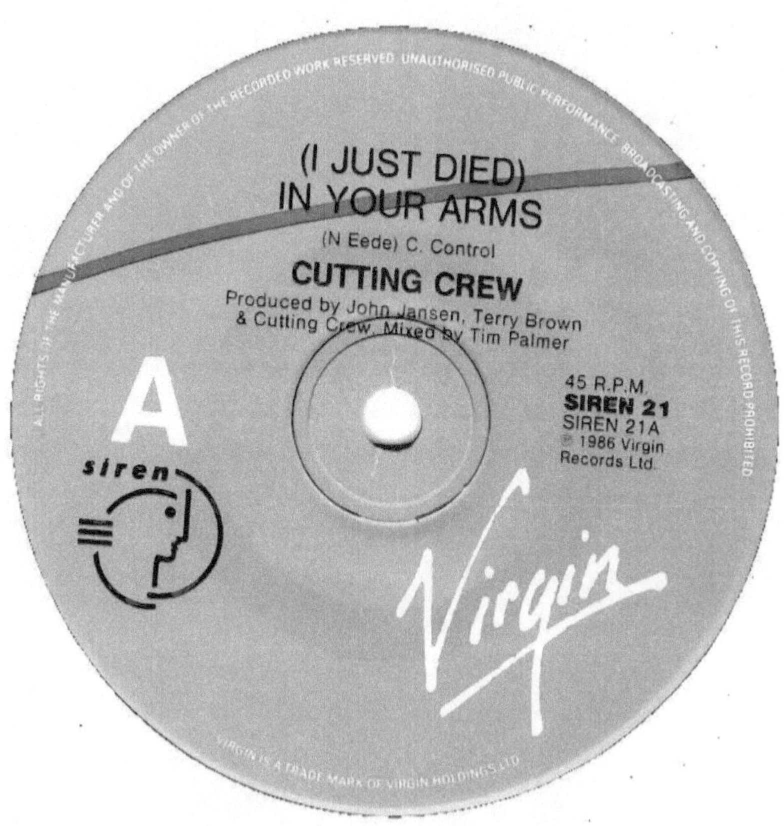# (I Just) Died in Your Arms
(Cutting Crew)
Siren/Virgin 1986

(I Just) Died in Your Arms is a song by the English pop rock band Cutting Crew, released as their debut single in July 1986 from their first studio album, *Broadcast*. The song was written by frontman Nick Van Eede, produced by Terry Brown, John Jansen and the band, and mixed at Utopia Studios in London by Tim Palmer.

(I Just) Died in Your Arms

Teresa Inge

Rhiannon Harper bobbed her head to the pulsing beat of "(I Just) Died in Your Arms" as she stocked vintage records in her bookstore, "Page & Vinyl," in North Carolina's Outer Banks.

Her sister, Layla, stepped out from behind a bookshelf. "Rhiannon, come look at this," she shouted, waving furiously toward the main window.

Rhiannon dropped the records in the bin. When she rounded the corner and glanced where her sister pointed, she noticed a black tour bus parked in front of the store. Four men dressed in black band t-shirts exited the bus.

"Oh-my-god, it's the Van Steel Band," she said as they walked toward her. Her voice held the same excitement as when she first listened to them as a teenager.

"Welcome to Page & Vinyl," she said, trying not to gush as they entered the store. "We specialize in rare finds and nostalgic classics. I'm Rhiannon, and this is my sister, Layla," she waved her hand toward her sister.

"Sounds like you two were named after famous rock songs?" The lead singer, Dexter Van Steel asked while standing near a bin of vintage records.

"Yes. Our parents loved rock music," added Layla. Her voice echoed her sister's excitement.

"What brings y'all to OBX? Layla asked. OBX refers to the Outer Banks, a group of coastal towns in the popular vacation destination.

"Our bus broke down on the way to our annual private gigs in Nags Head, and your sign caught our eye, so we stopped by," he said, introducing the band: bassist Colin Page, lead guitarist Kevin Scott, and drummer Marty Phelan.

"We know," the sisters said in unison as they tried to maintain their composure. Inside, however, both were fangirling over their unexpected visitors.

Dexter lifted one of the band's vinyl records from the bin. "I have an idea! We could organize a meet and greet and sign some of our records in your store while the radiator is repaired on our bus."

"That sounds good," Layla said. We have regular customers who would love to meet you, and your tour bus is already attracting a crowd." Pedestrians and bikers gathered beside the parked bus.

"We also have band t-shirts and memorabilia on the bus that we can sign," Colin added. "I can call our manager on the bus to bring them in."

"Great," Layla replied.

Colin reached for his cell phone. As he stepped away to talk, Rhiannon said, "Give us five minutes."

Her business sense took over. The sisters quickly set up a signing table with a "Van Steel Band" banner from Layla's vintage collection, and she announced the meet and greet on social media. As the band sat among nostalgic items, fans came in to meet them.

Within minutes, the band began autographing albums and talking about their glory days. When a fan mentioned a diary about them, Dexter's eyes lit up. "Ah, the infamous diary." He smacked the table with his palm, and the records jumped. "That's the stuff of legends."

Rhiannon's eyes widened. "What's in the diary?"

Dexter leaned in closer. "Juicy gossip and wild stories about our early tours. It was our ex-keyboard player's girlfriend's. She kept it on her bedside table and wrote down everything that happened at our '80s concerts. We're told its hidden in OBX, but we don't know where."

Rhiannon nudged her sister. A mystery was developing, and she wanted to be a part of it.

"We can try to find it before your tour is over here," Layla said.

"Before, I wanted it burned, but now it could be interesting," Dexter said, stroking his gray beard.

"Do you have other details about the diary?" Rhiannon asked.

Dexter sat back and crossed his arms. "It belonged to 'Sweet Connie,' a groupie. She lived here, but that was ages ago."

"Well, it seems we have a mystery to solve," Layla grinned.

"And we can start with the town's main historian, Mrs. Payton," Rhiannon said, looking up at the woman staring into their window with interest before walking away.

While their summer employee ran the Surfside Plaza store in Nags Head, a beach town, the sisters visited the coffee shop two doors down. Band posters lined the walls, and the aroma of coffee filled the air as Mrs. Payton enjoyed her decaf.

Rhiannon and Layla approached her. "We heard you might know someone named Connie who ran with a rock band in the '80s," Layla said.

Mrs. Payton's smile grew. "Oh yes, 'Sweet Connie.' She was the talk of the town."

"Do you know where we might find her?" Rhiannon asked.

Her finger tapped the table, and she took a sip of her coffee. "She left town years ago. But her cousin Tara lives here."

"Can you provide her contact info?" Layla asked.

Mrs. Payton settled herself in the chair. "Well, I don't give out people's private details," she said, "but Tara works at the Dare County Library in Kill Devil Hills."

"We'll check it out," Layla said, mapping their next steps.

It was a ten-minute drive from the coffee shop to the library located in the coastal town with a devilish name. Inside, it was easy to find Tara Lawrence by her name tag. She wore thick-rimmed glasses while shelving books.

The sisters approached her. "I'm Rhiannon Harper and this is my sister Layla. We would like to ask you about someone."

"Who is that?" Tara said, the annoyance clear in her voice.

"Connie," Rhiannon said.

"What do you want to know?"

"We heard she has a diary that we are interested in," Layla said.

Tara set the book down. "That diary's got more drama than a soap opera." She paused. "Aren't you two the owners of Page and Vinyl?"

"Yes, and we're fans of the band mentioned in the diary," Layla said.

Tara's expression softened. "Look. Connie died recently and left the diary to me. It's full of suggestive references, so I'm reluctant to revisit unpleasant memories for anyone," she said.

Rhiannon lowered her voice. "We get it, but we also feel that it could be a celebration of her life and the band's history."

Tara paused before replying. "Follow me." She led them to an office in the library and unlocked a desk drawer. She took out a leather-bound diary with yellowed pages. "I keep it here for reference. Here you go. Please interpret it carefully."

Rhiannon and Layla flipped through the pages, each one with vibrant writing. "This is so cool," said Layla, skimming stories of late-night jam sessions and wild parties.

"We'll take care of it," Rhiannon smiled toward Tara. "We plan to display it at the band's signing event at our store. Their tour bus broke down and they're meeting fans while it's fixed."

The sisters, now armed with the diary, rushed to "Page & Vinyl." As they entered the store, the men were still autographing and mingling with locals.

"You found it?" Dexter said.

Rhiannon lifted the diary as though it were a trophy. "A lucky break, thanks to Mrs. Payton and Tara." The buzz in the store was exciting. Fans rushed to buy rare '80s rock memorabilia bundled with merchandise.

As Rhiannon grabbed a display stand for the diary, she briefly scanned its pages.

Connie's diary was filled with tales of glamour, scandal, and rock 'n' roll adventures. Rhiannon ran her finger along a passage about a secret gig in OBX: "Marvin. If you are reading this, then the truth is out. Watch your back. – Connie."

"Look at this passage," Rhiannon showed Layla.

"What does that mean and who is Marvin?" Layla asked.

"I don't know but let's hide this away. We need to ask the band if they know a Marvin," Rhiannon said, tucking the diary beneath the counter.

Layla agreed, and a few minutes later, when there was a break in the signing activity, they made their way toward Dexter.

"Do you remember a fan named Marvin?" Layla asked.

Dexter's expression grew serious. "Marvin?" he repeated. "Why do you ask?"

"Connie made a note in the diary for Marvin to watch his back." Rhiannon handed him the diary, pointing toward the passage.

"Marvin was our roadie," he said. "He traveled with us on the first tour, and Connie documented it."

Shivers ran down Rhiannon's back. "Is he still around?"

"No, he left the business just after the tour. Haven't seen him since."

Rhiannon stared at her sister since they both loved mysteries but never expected one to appear in their store.

Hour after hour, the band autographed the last record and T-shirt on hand. Layla flipped the door sign to "CLOSED" and dimmed the lights except for a section in the back where the band sipped beers from a cooler from their bus. Around ten o'clock, noises of broken glass and raised voices were heard.

Rhiannon and Layla raced to the door and saw the tour bus window smashed. They made their way to the bus and spotted Kevin slumped over in the driver's seat. Rhiannon dropped down beside him, and he whispered to her, "Mar…" before he fell into her arms and grew listless.

Band members ran on board the bus in a state of shock. "Kevin," Dexter shouted.

"Call 911," Rhiannon told Layla. Layla grabbed her cell in a trembling hand and dialed.

Rhiannon looked at the band. "The cops will be here soon. Did any of you see anything?"

Colin, the bassist, spoke up. "We were all inside until we heard the crash."

"He said 'Mar…'" just before he died," Rhiannon said.

Dexter was pale as he caught the words. "Marvin? It can't be…"

Sirens wailed in the distance.

Rhiannon spotted a small, leather booklet like the diary, just beyond the broken glass. Layla, grab that," she whispered, motioning at the item. "It might be important."

Layla grabbed the booklet and stuffed it in her pocket.

Moments later, blue, and red lights lit up the night as the police arrived. The police shoved their way through the crowd to evaluate the situation and tape off the scene.

"This is no joke," Layla said quietly to Rhiannon. "What if Marvin is here?"

"We need to be careful," Rhiannon said. "Let's tell the police about the vandalism and what Kevin said before dying in my arms."

The next few hours became a flurry of questions as the band huddled outside. The cheers of the signing had turned into a solemn vigil, with whispers from concerned fans standing behind the yellow crime scene tape the police had erected.

After being questioned, the sisters went to their shared living space in the back of the store. "We can't just sit here," Layla said, pacing the floor. "We have to do something."

"Let's read the booklet." Rhiannon grabbed the ragged book.

"What does it say?" Layla asked.

"There are details about a theft and her suspicion that Marvin stole money from the band, a secret she kept, to avoid trouble. Later she confronted him, and he promised revenge."

"We need to see if Marvin is still around. He could be a suspect."

"But why would he wait so long for revenge and why did she mention in the diary to watch his back?" Layla asked.

"Maybe he heard about the special gigs and Connie had uncovered more details," Rhiannon said. "We probably should talk to Tara again, find out if she's heard anything."

The following morning, the sisters visited the library as the sun kissed the coastal town. Tara was taken aback when they arrived. "Did you get what you wanted?" she asked.

"We got more than we asked for," Layla added. "Kevin was murdered last night."

Tara's hand flew to her mouth. "What happened?"

Rhiannon held out the booklet. "We suspect it may be related to this," she said. "Connie wrote about Marvin, a band roadie who ripped off the band."

Tara grabbed the booklet, running her finger across the page. "Yes, I remember Marvin. He was always looking to make his next score."

Rhiannon leaned forward. "Do you know where he is?"

"No. He was a drifter. But I do remember he had a cousin, Marcus, who had a boat."

"Do you know where we can find Marcus?" Layla asked.

"He lives in a cottage near the Manteo marina," she said. "But Marcus doesn't like company."

Moments later, the sisters drove to the marina in the quaint waterfront town. The smell of salt in the air washed over the rows of boats floating calmly in the water. Marcus's cottage stood out, a worn blue '80s relic with a small fishing boat next to it. Rhiannon knocked on the door. It was opened by a stocky man, his eyes narrowing in on their appearance. "What do you two want?" he barked.

"We're here for Marcus," Layla said, keeping her voice even despite the man's aggressive tone. "We have some questions about his cousin, Marvin."

"What do you want with Marvin?" He kept his hand on the door, as though ready to slam it. Rhiannon held up the diary. "We found this," she said. "It belonged to Connie. She had a few things to say about Marvin, which are important."

Marcus's hold on the door slackened. "Connie," he said. "What kind of things?"

"Some serious allegations," Rhiannon said. "We're guessing it might have something to do with Kevin last night."

"Like what?"

"Money stolen from the band," Rhiannon said, studying his expression. Marcus stepped away from the door, letting the sisters inside the cramped cottage filled with fishing gear. "Marvin was always a sneaky son-of-a-gun," he said, rubbing his beard. "What's in that diary of hers?"

Layla intervened. "It's about Connie's life with the band," she said. "It suggests Marvin cheated them, and she planned to expose him."

"Marvin never could be trusted," he said, getting the diary from Rhiannon. "What happened to her?"

"She died recently," Rhiannon said. "But before she died, she left the diary with her cousin Tara."

"I didn't know," he said, thumbing through the pages and entries.

"We just want to solve Kevin's murder," Rhiannon said. "If Marvin had a motive, it's quite possible that it might be related."

"Do you know where Marvin is now?" Layla asked.

Marcus closed the diary. "I haven't talked to him in years."

"We need to track him down," Layla said. "We don't want to presume he's guilty without speaking to him."

"I can give you the last address I have for him," Marcus said, reaching into a drawer and pulling out a battered notebook. He scribbled something on a slip of paper and gave it to them. The sisters thanked Marcus and left with the diary and booklet.

The sisters drove to a rundown warehouse near Manteo. Windows were covered in plywood, and the metal siding was rusted.

"This can't be right," Layla said, as they approached the building.

"It's worth checking out." Rhiannon pulled the car to a stop, and they walked to the building. The front door was ajar, so they pushed it open. The room had dusty boxes and old furniture. But it was a man in a corner armchair with his back to them that kept them looking. He was middle-aged, with a greasy ponytail and a beer gut spilling over a faded band t-shirt. As they came closer, they spotted a knife in his hand.

"Marvin?" Rhiannon whispered, her heart racing. The man lifted his head and turned swiftly.

"We're not here to harm you," Layla said. "We just need to talk."

Marvin's eyes flicked from the sisters to the knife. "You're here about the diary, aren't you?"

"We just want the truth," Rhiannon said. "Connie's diary said you'd had a falling out with the band. What happened?"

"They painted me a thief, and they stole my job, my friends, my life on the road." He hesitated, as Layla adjusted the diary in her hand. "And then Connie had to write about me in her diary as if I was a joke."

"Kevin is dead, and we need to find out why," Layla said.

"Kevin?" He spat out the name. "He was too good to get his hands dirty. But he knew what they did to me."

Rhiannon glanced at her sister, realizing they had found more than they'd bargained for.

"Marvin, we have to go to the police," Layla said. "They will want to hear your story."

Marvin's eyes flashed a look of desperation. At last, he placed the knife on the table. "I have been running for years, so maybe I need to visit them."

"We'll go with you and make sure your voice is heard," Rhiannon said. The sisters stayed calm as they took Marvin, the diary and booklet to the police station. Layla called ahead and told them they had a suspect in Kevin's murder who was willing to come in for questioning.

"Tell me everything," Detective Reynolds pointed to a cramped interrogation room. Marvin sank into the chair with the sisters beside him. He told them about the money theft and working with the band.

Detective Reynolds took notes as Marvin talked. "And you didn't kill Kevin?" she asked.

"I had my arguments with him, but I didn't kill him."

"We must verify your story. But right now, I'm holding you for further questioning."

The sisters were left to watch as Marvin was taken away. They felt a mixture of pity and fear and knew they had awakened something dark and twisted.

"Do you think he's telling the truth?" Layla asked.

"Maybe." Rhiannon stared at the closed interrogation room door. "If so, we still have a murderer amongst us."

The detective grabbed her notes. "We'll look into your information. But we need more than a diary entry to arrest."

"Let's keep searching," Rhiannon said, driving Layla to the store from the police station.

"We can start by talking to the band again. I think they're holding out on us," Layla said as they pulled into the Page & Vinyl parking lot.

The band stood outside of the broken-down bus as the sisters approached. "What happened to Marvin?" asked Dexter.

Rhiannon let her gaze drift to the diary. "He didn't admit to killing Kevin, but he has a motive."

An awkward silence filled the air. "What do we do now?" he asked.

"Let's talk," Rhiannon nodded toward the bus. "There's something we need to know."

Once they sat down, the ladies filled the band in on what Marvin said about the stolen money. "We knew something was going on with Marvin," Dexter said, "but we didn't know it was that deep."

Layla leaned forward. "What happened at the secret gig?"

Marty, the drummer, spoke up. "We were a young band just coming into fame. The private party was for a big-wig record producer set up by Marvin after he was fired. But we let him talk us into doing the gig because of the producer."

"And what happened?" Rhiannon asked.

"When we met the client, he said he paid Marvin for the booking but only hired us as a favor to Marvin for revenge after we fired him, so we wouldn't be paid."

"And Connie was about to expose this?" Layla asked.

"She had the diary, and it would ruin our reputation if it got out, "Dexter said.

"And the next day after the murder?" Rhiannon pressed.

"That night, we had a falling out with Kevin," Colin, the bassist, said. "We found out he was using drugs again."

A shiver ran down Rhiannon's spine. "Then what happened?"

"There were some heated moments," Marty, offered. "But we decided to give Kevin another chance to get help."

"Why was Marvin fired?" Layla asked.

"He was constantly late to gigs," Dexter said.

When Rhiannon stepped off the bus with her sister, she had the unsettling feeling they hadn't connected all the dots. As the sun dipped toward OBX, they met in their office, an open page of the diary and book between them.

"There's an entry that we haven't read yet." Layla pointed to a page marked with a faded Post-it note.

Rhiannon read the final words aloud. "The gig was a sting," it said. Somebody had hired Marvin to smear the group, and steal cash from the special gig."

"We were so focused on Marvin's vendetta that we didn't even think about anybody else," Layla said.

"We have to figure out who it is," Layla said. "Let's go over the diary again," Rhiannon flipped through the pages. "There must be a link to Marvin and the murderer."

"Here's something." Layla pointed toward the name Marcus, scrawled in the margin of a page.

Rhiannon's eyes lit up. "Marcus," she repeated. "Could he be the one?"

"Kevin did say Mar… before he died. "Perhaps he was referring to Marcus," Layla said.

They opted to visit Marcus one more time. Rhiannon knocked on the door. Marcus opened it. "What do you want?"

"The truth," Layla said. "Why did you set Marvin up?"

"Marvin wanted to play with the big boys, but he didn't know when to keep his mouth shut."

"And Kevin knew?" Rhiannon asked.

"When Kevin was involved with Connie, she gave him the booklet mentioning Marvin's special gig payment. He threatened Marvin and me for drug money, so he had to be silenced."

"And you killed him?" Layla asked.

"I didn't want to, but it was him or me. And I sure wasn't going to let a washed-up rockstar ruin everything that I'd put together."

"You can't get away with this," Layla said, her voice trembling.

"Who's going to stop me?" His hand patted a gun wedged in the waistband of his jeans.

"We need to tell the police," Rhiannon said.

Marcus laughed. "You tell the cops Marvin killed him, and then you and the band won't end up like Kevin."

Fear gripped Rhiannon. But she couldn't let Marcus get away with murder. "Okay," she lied.

"Good choice," Marcus said. "You have until tomorrow." He closed the door in their faces.

Rhiannon and Layla fled the cottage to tell the band. The bus was parked in the same spot near their store.

"What's going on?" Dexter asked as the sisters boarded the bus.

"We found out who killed Kevin," Rhiannon said.

"Who was it?" Colin asked.

Rhiannon held up the diary. "Marcus," she said. "He's been playing us all. We need to tell the police."

"We'll go with you," Dexter said.

"Let's go. But we need to be cautious. Marcus is dangerous," Rhiannon said.

They crammed into the sisters' car and drove to the station, diary, and booklet in hand. The detective heard their story in the interrogation room. "This is big," she said.

"Marcus killed Kevin," Rhiannon said.

The detective hesitated for a moment. "All right," she said, standing up. "We'll go get him."

Over the next two days, the sisters shared their account with the police and media. Although the bus was repaired, they asked the band to stay an extra day to meet Tara, Mrs. Payton, and reconnect with Marvin.

"I'm glad they got Marcus, though his death was tragic," Tara said as she drank wine with Rhiannon, Layla, and Mrs. Payton.

"And Connie probably learned about Marcus, which would explain her cryptic note in the diary to Marvin," Layla said.

Rhiannon looked at the band, full of laughter, in the back of the store with Marvin over a beer. She concluded that Marvin must have feared Marcus. Everyone agreed that Connie's diary and booklet would be returned to Tara and remain locked in the drawer.

Black Velvet
(Alannah Myles)
Atlantic Records 1989

Black Velvet is a song written by Canadian songwriters Christopher Ward and David Tyson and performed by Canadian singer-songwriter Alannah Myles. It was released in July 1989 as the second single from Myles' first studio album, *Alannah Myles*, by Atlantic Records. It became a #1 hit on the US Billboard Hot 100, #10 in Canada and #2 in the UK. The power ballad[5] also reached number one in Norway, Sweden, and Switzerland and was a major success in several other countries.

Black Velvet

Michael Bracken

Rufus Hoyt had been standing in the Marathon service station lot, staring at a black-velvet Elvis for nearly ten minutes before Elmer Witherspoon finished pumping gas into his 1967 Chevelle and joined him. Elvis hung amidst paintings of Dale Earnhardt, John Wayne, and Jesus, and in it he wore a white jumpsuit open to his belly button, had a red scarf around his neck, and held a microphone in his right hand. His mouth was open as if caught in mid song.

"Damn, that's beautiful," Rufus said. "Elvis ain't looked that good in years."

Elmer stared at his best friend. "Course not. He's dead."

Chewing tobacco, an overweight blonde with more fingers than teeth sat behind a folding card table, protecting a metal cash box and a credit card machine. She eyed both men, once with her good eye and once with her lazy eye. As Rufus approached, she said, "Yeah?"

"How much for the Elvis?"

"A hundred and nine fifty," she said. Her voice sounded like a two-pack-a-day habit had mated with a cement truck. "A hundred even if you pay cash."

Rufus pulled out his wallet and started counting presidents. After a moment, he turned to Elmer. "I ain't got enough. Can you—"

"I'm not helping you buy one of those things," Elmer said. "You already have enough crap in that trailer of yours."

Rufus turned to the woman. "Would you take eighty-seven?"

"Sonny," she said. "I offered you a cash discount, and now you're trying to shake me down."

"But—"

"Go on. Git!" She made a brushing motion with her hand. "I got other customers."

Even though there were no other customers, Elmer grabbed Rufus's arm and encouraged him to leave. Disappointed, Rufus shuffled toward Elmer's Chevelle.

Once they were settled into the car and Elmer was pulling out of the Marathon station onto Main Street, he said, "I know where we can find an original."

"An original what?"

"Painting on black velvet. Not one of those mass-produced replicas."

"Elvis?"

"Yep."

"That would be worth a mint," Rufus said. He turned to Elmer. "Where?"

"Memphis."

"You don't mean Graceland, do you?"

"Oh, hell no. Another place."

When Elmer wouldn't tell him where, Rufus turned around and dug through the 8-track tapes littering the rear seat. After he found the one he wanted, he said, "Too bad all your tapes ain't worth anything."

Before Elmer could respond, Elvis's "Love Me Tender" filled the car.

Rufus's eyes watered. "I used to sing this to Alannah when we were dating."

Elmer pressed the fast forward button to one of Elvis's rocking songs. Then they rolled down the car windows and sang along all the way back to Rufus's single-wide mobile home.

* * *

Elmer had not been wrong when he had described Rufus's home as being filled with crap. Rufus had Beanie Babies, Cabbage Patch Kids, and Pet Rocks, some in their original packaging but most not. He also had G.I. Joes and Barbies and Star Wars figurines and all manner of other toys that might have had greater value if still in the original packaging, none of it organized in any obvious fashion. He called himself a collector—his ex-wife called him a hoarder—but he made just enough money buying and selling collectables to keep the electricity on and beer in the fridge.

Rufus pointed to the living room wall behind the sofa, where it was obvious a large painting had been removed. "Alannah took Jesus."

"And you want to put up Elvis in his place?"

"Nobody else is deserving."

Elmer shook his head, made his way to the kitchen, and helped himself to a bottle of Budweiser from the icebox. He opened it and leaned against the kitchen counter.

Rufus was right behind him and opened his own bottle of beer. "You going to tell me about that black-velvet painting up in Memphis?"

Elmer took a long draw from his beer bottle. "I was working up there two summers ago, when this whole state was in the middle of a dry spell, and I couldn't find no work local. One night after working the dinner rush washing dishes at the Peabody, I was walking on Beale Street, listening to the music coming out of all the clubs like some kind of heat wave, and I stopped to stare at the Elvis statue over there close to B.B. King's Blues Club. I'd been standing there, I don't know, maybe five minutes, and this guy walks up to me and asks if I'm a fan."

Rufus interrupted. "Who ain't?"

"That's what I told him. Elvis was the alpha and the omega, the beginning and the end of rock'n'roll. There will never be anyone like him again."

"Amen."

"And he said to me, this man I had never seen before in my life, that he has something no one else has."

"Which was?"

"An original Edgar Leeteg Elvis on black velvet," Elmer said.

"Really? A Leeteg? Ain't he the man who made painting on black velvet popular? Didn't he mostly paint Polynesian women with their tits hanging out?" Rufus asked. "So? Did you see it, the Elvis?"

Elmer nodded. "I did. He took me back to his place and showed me a room full of paintings he said were by Leeteg. I know about as much about the value of black-velvet paintings as you know about quantum physics, but he swore every one of them was worth several thousand dollars to the right collector."

"They are. I know a guy down in Jackson, runs a place named Black Velvet, If You Please, who would buy it, no questions asked," Rufus said. "That Elvis might be worth tens of thousands."

"Yeah?"

"So, what happened?"

"What happened is that I realized why he'd invited me back to his place, and it wasn't just to see his paintings. I excused myself and got the hell out of there."

* * *

Elmer spent the next day bussing tables and washing dishes at Grits, the only diner in town to regularly fail health inspections and remain open. At the end of the day, he opened that week's pay envelope, compared the amount he had earned after deductions to the unpaid bills littering the top of his dining room table, and returned to Rufus's single-wide. As soon as his friend opened the door, he said, "Let's do it. Let's go get that Elvis."

"All the way to Memphis?"

"I'll buy the gas, you bring those Budweisers from your fridge."

Rufus belched. "I drank 'em all."

Elmer waved a hand in front of his face to redirect the stench of Rufus's breath. "Fine. We'll stop at the Marathon on the way out of town. While I get gas, you can buy more beer."

* * *

Three hours later, they rolled into Memphis, and soon they were cruising Beale Street, windows open, listening to the music drifting out of the various barrooms and night clubs.

"That's where I met him," Elmer said as he slowed his Chevelle and pointed at the giant bronze statue in Elvis Presley Plaza. He ignored the honking car behind him and slowed even more. "I miss Elvis. Music just hasn't been the same since he passed."

Rufus nudged him. "Get a move on. Where's this house where you saw the painting?"

"I'm pretty sure it's this way." Elmer turned at the next intersection and the honking horn ceased. He drove south from Beale Street, finally leaving the business district behind and entering a neighborhood of older two-story houses that had once been home to the city's elite. Now most of them had been subdivided into multi-tenant dwellings. Mid-block, he pulled to the curb and indicated one of the homes.

"He brought you all the way out here to show you his Elvis painting?"

"That's what I thought," Elmer said. "I had to walk most of the way back when I realized what he really wanted to show me. That's why I remember how to find this place."

"So, where are they? The paintings?"

"Second floor, front left bedroom."

"And you said he's rich?"

"Well, he ain't living in a subdivide. That entire house is his."

Rufus looked at it again. Though not in much better shape than the properties around it, that it remained a single-family home indicated the owner retained some level of financial stability. He tapped Elmer's shoulder. "Drive away before we look suspicious. We'll come back when it gets dark."

* * *

By the time Rufus and Elmer returned to the house containing the Elvis painting, they had consumed all the beer they'd brought north from Mississippi and an additional twelve-pack they'd picked up after their stop at a hardware store. They drove around the block and down the alley behind the house, confirming there were no lights on inside.

Elmer parked next to a Mercedes in a carport behind the house, and he unscrewed the car's interior light before opening the door. The rear gate was unlocked and a moment later they stood on the back porch. Elmer looked for evidence of an alarm system, didn't see any, and popped the lock. Then they were inside, and they moved slowly up the stairs to the front left bedroom on the second floor.

The beam of light from the flashlight they'd purchased earlier washed over all manner of Polynesian women until it finally settled on a young Elvis, tussled hair hanging over his forehead, sideburns not as long as they would later become, smiling that little boy's smile that made women swoon.

"That's a beauty," Rufus whispered.

He helped Elmer take the painting off the wall, and Elmer carried it into the hall.

As the passed the bathroom, Rufus whispered, "I got to go. All that beer we drank wants out."

"Well, hurry up."

He did.

"But don't flu—"

The flush of the toilet and the rumble of the old house's pipes made enough noise to wake tenants in the next building. As Rufus zipped up, they heard, "What the hell are you two doing?"

Elmer spun around to face the painting's owner, the same portly man who had invited him to the house the first time he had visited. He wore pajamas imprinted with Elvis's face and he held a snub-nosed .32 pointed at them. Elmer said, "We're taking Elvis."

"Not if I shoot you first."

Rufus said, "You didn't tell me he had a gun."

"I didn't know." Elmer shifted position so the painting was between him and the revolver's barrel. Elvis wouldn't protect them if the man squeezed the trigger, but perhaps the painting's owner might think twice about damaging Elvis, especially if the painting was worth what Elmer believed it was.

From behind Elmer, Rufus threw the flashlight, the spinning light briefly illuminating another room containing an easel holding partially completed painting of a topless Tahitian woman. It struck the portly man's forehead, surprising him, and causing him to squeeze the .32's trigger as he fell. The bullet went wide, ricocheting off the clawfoot bathtub and shattering the mirror.

Awkwardly, because he still held the black-velvet painting, Elmer hurried forward and kicked the .32 out of the man's hand. It clattered down the staircase.

"Tie him up," Elmer told Rufus.

"With what?"

"Find something. Just tie him up while I take this out to the car."

Rufus grabbed the collar of the man's pajama shirt and dragged him into the bedroom as Elmer headed down the stairs with the painting. Elmer had just slid it into the back seat of his Chevelle when Rufus joined him.

"I handcuffed him to his headboard."

"You what?"

"He had fur-lined handcuffs on his nightstand, so I used 'em."

Elmer shook his head, climbed into his car, and started the engine as Rufus climbed into the passenger seat. Before long they were headed south on Interstate 55, Elvis blaring through the 8-track system.

* * *

Later that day, they arrived in Jackson, found Black Velvet, If You Please, and waited a half block away from the hole-in-the-wall art gallery until a dour man wearing gold-rimmed eyeglasses arrived and unlocked the front door. He had barely turned on the lights when they entered the shop, Rufus leading the way because he knew Mr. Myles. Behind him, Elmer struggled to get the stolen painting through the door.

The place wasn't much bigger than a shipping container, though the ceiling was at least twice the height of one, and the walls were covered with a variety of black-velvet paintings depicting all manner of subjects.

Myles asked, "Been a long time, Rufus. You here about the Beanie Babies in original packaging I called you about last week?"

"Nah. We got us an original Leeteg," Rufus told the man. "It's worth thousands, but we just want—"

"Thousands? Most of his originals don't sell for more than a few hundred dollars, so it would have to be something special—"

"It is." Rufus turned. "Show him."

Elmer turned the stolen painting around so the shop's owner could see it. Myles glanced at it and snorted with derision. "That's a fake."

"It can't be." Elmer pointed at the artist's signature. "He signed it and everything."

"You two are dumber than a box of pet rocks," the shop owner said. He flipped the painting over, examined something on the frame, then returned the painting to Elmer. "Edgar Leeteg couldn't have painted Elvis unless he was a time-traveler. He died in February nineteen-fifty-three, months before Elvis's first recording."

"So, this is—?"

"Not worth the gas it took to get it here."

Elmer and Rufus looked at each other.

"I can sell you an authentic Leeteg painting or even an original Velvis by Miguel Mariscal, if you want, but this"—Myles waved his hand at the Elvis painting—"is stinking up my gallery. You'd best get it on out of here."

A few minutes later, Elmer carried the painting back to his Chevelle and Rufus carried three Beanie Babies still in their original packaging. They cost him most of what he had set aside for that month's trailer payment.

Elmer drove to Rufus's single-wide in silence. He wouldn't even let Rufus play one of the Elvis 8-track tapes.

Rufus dumped the Beanie Babies on the coffee table table, then hung the black-velvet painting over his couch, where the painting of Jesus had hung until his ex-wife took it.

"Looks good," Elmer said, "but maybe I should have just given you the money to buy the one at the Marathon station."

An unfamiliar man's voice said, "Maybe you should have."

Elmer and Rufus turned to see the portly man from Memphis standing in the open doorway, a bruise on his forehead and his snub-nosed .32 in one hand. Dressed, he appeared far more imposing than he had when they encountered him in his home.

"I want my Elvis back."

"Why? It ain't worth anything," Elmer said.

Rufus asked, "How did you—?"

"Myles called me. He recognized my mark on the picture frame."

When Elmer stepped toward him, the portly man squeezed the revolver's trigger. The bullet ricocheted off a Batman lunchbox and drilled a hole through Elvis's forehead.

Wide-eyed, Rufus exclaimed, "You shot Elvis!"

"That could have been you."

"Why do you want the painting back?" Elmer asked. "It's a fake."

"With a hole in it," Rufus added.

"It took me years to master Leeteg's signature."

Rufus and Elmer looked at the bottom corner of the Elvis painting, where someone had painted the artist's signature in block letters: LEETEG TAHITI ©.

Elmer said, "That's not a signature. That's something a kindergartener would do."

The portly man motioned with the barrel of the revolver. "Move over there by the stack of *Partridge Family* thermoses and get on your knees."

After they were on their knees, Elmer told Rufus, "Bet you wish your ex hadn't taken Jesus. If he were here, you could pray to him."

"I'll pray to Elvis. He'll save us."

The portly man looked at Elmer. "Your friend isn't right in the head."

Elmer shrugged. The portly man wasn't wrong.

While keeping the .32 pointed in the general direction of the two men kneeling on the floor, the portly man stepped toward the couch. He stumbled on a pile of Tickle Me Elmos, and the entire pile giggled as he dropped to his ass on the couch. "What is all this crap?"

Elmer nodded at his friend. "Rufus sells collectibles."

"They aren't even in their original packaging."

"Don't matter," Rufus said. "People want what they want."

"Like that Elvis," Elmer said. "What's special about it?"

"Nothing." The portly man glanced up at the painting. "I have a dozen more in my storeroom."

"Then why did you come looking for this one?"

"Myles sells a lot of my work, but he won't take any of my Velvises, and he—"

Elmer interrupted. He remembered the easel and unfinished painting he'd glimpsed in the spinning light when Rufus had thrown his flashlight into the portly man's forehead the previous night. "You're painting counterfeit Leetegs."

"And Miguel Mariscals as well," the portly man added. "I tried to combine the two, but Myles tells me knowledgeable buyers will recognize Leeteg's Velvises as fakes. He insisted I stop, but I'd already painted thirteen of them." He shook his head and indicated the painting on the wall behind him. "This one was my best—I nailed the artist's signature on this one—so I had it hanging in my gallery until you two took it."

Elmer glanced at Rufus, realized his friend was mouthing the words to "Love Me Tender" as if it were a prayer, and said, "Elvis isn't worth dying for, and my knees are killing me."

He used the coffee table to leverage himself to his feet. The barrel of the portly man's .32 tracked his movements.

"Take your painting," Elmer said. "We won't stop you. Hell, I'll help you carry it out."

"That isn't enough. You broke into my house, shattered my bathroom mirror, handcuffed me to my bed, and stole my painting, which now has a hole in it."

Elmer didn't point out that both the shattered bathroom window and the hole in Elvis's forehead was the result of the portly man's poor aim. "If we had any money, we wouldn't have stolen the painting and tried to sell it."

The portly man indicated the three packaged Beanie Babies on the coffee table. "Those. And what else do you have that I might be able to monetize?"

Elmer turned to Rufus, who stopped reciting "Love Me Tender" and looked up.

"He has some Cabbage Patch Kids in original packaging and a couple of Furbys, too."

"Get them. Don't do anything stupid or I'll shoot your friend."

Elmer didn't expect the portly man to actually shoot Rufus, but a ricochet off any of the junk in Rufus's single-wide could hit either of them. He collected two Cabbage Patch Kids and four Furbys from one of the bedrooms and dumped them on the coffee table with the Beanie Babies. He nudged Rufus with his toe. "You got a bag?"

"Under the sink."

A moment later, Elmer had bagged the collectables and handed them to Rufus. The portly man rose from the couch, moved to the doorway, and motioned to Elmer. "You get Elvis."

Elmer took the painting from the wall as Rufus pushed himself to his feet. They carried the portly man's loot outside to his Mercedes, which had been parked on the far side of Elmer's Chevelle, and Elmer put Elvis in the back seat of the Mercedes. As he backed out of the car, Rufus swung the collectibles-filled trash bag at the portly man, hitting his right arm and causing him to squeeze the .32's trigger. The bullet drilled a hole through the Chevelle's rear quarter panel.

"Damn it, Rufus!"

The portly man swung the revolver around and pointed it at Elmer.

He held up his hands, palms forward, to placate the man. Then he picked up the bag of collectibles, tossed it in the rear seat of the Mercedes, and closed the door.

The portly man opened the driver's door. He started, "If I ever see either of you again—"

"—it'll be too soon," Elmer finished.

A moment later, the Mercedes drove away.

Rufus turned to Elmer. "You gave him my best stuff," insisted. "And my Elvis!"

"You're lucky he didn't shoot you. Hell, you're lucky I don't shoot you now."

They returned to the living room and started at the hole in the paneling where Elvis's forehead had been.

Elmer turned to Rufus. "You have any beer?"

He didn't have. They had finished it the day before, and they didn't have any left from their stop on the way to Jackson. Elmer suggested a trip to the Marathon station.

* * *

The overweight blonde with more fingers than teeth had set up at the service station again. While Elmer went inside to purchase a thirty-six-pack of Budweiser, Rufus wandered over to her display to examine the various black-velvet paintings. The selection was different than before, but still heavy on Dale Earnhardt, John Wayne, Jesus, and Elvis.

When Elmer joined him, Rufus was standing in front of a painting of Elvis in his sparkly white jumpsuit. Elvis stood with his arms outstretched, a microphone in his right hand, a red scarf in his left, and a crown of thorns over his pompadour.

"You going to stare at it until your eyes bleed?" the woman asked. Her voice still sounded like a two-pack-a-day habit had mated with a cement truck.

Rufus turned to Elmer. "I need something to cover the hole in my wall," he said, "and you owe me for all the stuff you gave away."

Elmer still had available funds on his MasterCard, so he asked the woman the painting's price.

She narrowed her eyes. "Two twenty-nine. Two twenty if you pay cash."

"That's more than double what you wanted for the one we asked about the other day."

"Yeah, but this one's an original Mariscal."

Elmer doubted it. An original Mariscal wouldn't be for sale on a street corner. And he'd just had a bad experience dealing with a counterfeiter.

"I want this one," Rufus said.

Elmer handed his credit card to the woman, collected the receipt and the painting a moment later, and drove to Rufus's double-wide with it in the rear seat of his Chevelle. They hung it on Rufus's living-room wall, hiding the bullet hole, then drank Budweiser while "Love Me Tender" played repeatedly on the stereo and the sun slowly set in a molasses-colored sky.

Roll to Me
(Del Amitri)
A&M 1995

Roll to Me is a song by Scottish pop rock band Del Amitri, released as the third single from their fourth studio album, *Twisted* (1995). The song became their biggest hit in the United States when it reached #10 on the Billboard Hot 100 chart. It finished at #55 on the Billboard Year-End Hot 100 singles chart of 1995. In the United Kingdom, it was a moderate hit, peaking at #22 on the UK Singles Chart.

Roll to Me

Mary Dutta

Cecile Henderson rang the video doorbell her daughter had installed after the whole kerfuffle over returning her set of keys.

She smiled as Esme opened the door a crack. Esme did not return the smile.

"I know I'm supposed to call," Cecile said, brandishing a bakery box, "but I brought goodies."

Her daughter stood in the door until Cecile's smile faltered, then swung it open. "Okay, you can come in and get that box as long as you're here."

Cecile knew she wouldn't have been invited in if Logan had been home. That's why she had waited down the block until she saw him drive away.

"I got your mail, too," she called after her daughter's retreating back.

Esme turned and snatched the envelopes sticking out of Cecile's bag. "That's an invasion of privacy, mother."

"Fine," Cecile said with an exaggerated sigh, "I won't touch your junk mail. I was just trying to help." She centered the cardboard box on the kitchen island's empty expanse. Esme should keep a bowl of fruit out. And a decorative napkin holder.

"Why are you bringing me baked goods? You know we cut out white sugar."

"I thought I could tempt you with something from that new French bakery." Cecile opened the box and pushed it toward her. "Go on,

Logan will never know."

Esme pushed the box back toward Cecile. "Logan doesn't control what I eat. I do."

"But you always had such a sweet tooth as a kid."

"Yes, but I'm not a kid anymore."

As if Cecile could forget. Nowadays, Logan had Esme eating things like harissa and gochujang. Every exotic item he added to the menu was just one more bit of evidence that he was the wrong guy for her daughter.

Esme shook her head and reached for the garage door. "I'll get the box. Wait here."

Cecile took a seat on one of the island's metal stools. Logan must have chosen the backless style. Esme had always struggled with her posture.

She watched the digital photo frame on the opposite counter cycle through images of the supposedly happy couple. She didn't really expect any pictures of herself to pop up, but couldn't suppress a surge of disappointment when she was proved right.

She shifted her gaze to Logan's training calendar, stuck to the refrigerator with a souvenir magnet from Vietnam. Esme had never traveled out of the country until Logan started dragging her around the world. It looked like the only place he was going for the next couple of months, however, were local mountain bike trails. At least he hasn't roped her daughter into that dangerous hobby. Cecile snapped a picture, figuring it couldn't hurt to know when he wasn't going to be home.

Esme returned with a cardboard box and deposited it in front of her mother. Cecile opened the flaps. A Dresden shepherdess stared accusingly at her.

"You loved these figurines at grandma's," she said. "Are you sure you don't want them?"

She couldn't believe that Esme preferred her home's minimalist décor to a display of family heirlooms.

"Absolutely sure, and now I really need to get back to work." Esme closed the flaps and lifted the box. "I'll carry this out to your car for you."

Cecile picked up her rejected madeleines and followed her. She opened the rear door of her car and stepped back for Esme to load her grandmother's spurned treasures.

"What's with the binoculars?" Esme said. Cecile had forgotten she had left them on the back seat.

"I've taken up bird watching."

Esme finally smiled. "That's good. It's healthy to find new interests." She slammed the door and stepped back instead of reaching for a hug. "I'll see you at Julia's wedding," she said, and headed back into her house.

Cecile stared at the closed door for a few minutes, hoping her daughter might reappear, then drove away.

Her bakery offerings found a more appreciative audience in her book group that evening, but they were less pleased with her opinions. Cecile fidgeted as everyone else gushed over that month's selection, a novel about a young woman's coming of age.

"The daughter character talks a lot about boundaries," she said, "but a mother's love knows no bounds. She doesn't appreciate that."

The group members exchanged glances, and one eyeroll.

"I think," the woman on her left said, "the story is about how we need to love people for who they truly are, not what we want them to be."

Cecile ignored her. She knew her daughter had gone off to Paris to study abroad and they hadn't seen each other for four months. What could that woman know about a mother's love?

She fumed wordlessly for the rest of the meeting. As the other women headed into the night, her host pulled her aside. "I meant to tell you I bumped into Esme and her partner at the farmer's market last weekend. She seems to be doing great."

Cecile had to admit that her daughter certainly *seemed* happy. But she just couldn't believe that the life Esme was living with Logan was everything she had hoped it would be. It certainly wasn't what Cecile had hoped for her.

Later that night, she sat in Esme's room, as she did every evening before bed. The ruffled bedspread and rose wallpaper Cecile had chosen for her little girl with such delight remained untouched. For those few minutes every day, she pretended that nothing else had changed either.

She had abandoned her other evening activity: stalking Logan online. Despite her best efforts, she could find nothing that would convince her daughter to leave him. He had a successful career. He never posted anything objectionable on social media. He had promptly deleted his profile from the dating app where they met. There were no incriminating pictures out there, just shots of him placing in mountain bike races and winning awards for volunteering.

Cecile still hoped her in-person surveillance might pan out, although she worried that Logan might have spotted her a couple of times. She hadn't caught him doing anything suspicious. Not yet, anyway. He met friends for drinks and behaved appropriately with the women. He ran mundane errands to the grocery store and dry cleaner. When she tracked his solo biking adventures through her binoculars he simply rolled along without incident.

Of course, keeping an eye on Logan sometimes meant keeping an eye on Esme as well. Cecile didn't recognize this version of her daughter. She had a circle of friends Cecile knew nothing about, and a range of activities she had never enjoyed before. Things like kayaking and shopping for goat-milk soap. Her Esme was disappearing before her eyes and Cecile refused to accept that her daughter was happy about it.

The old Esme made an appearance at her cousin Julia's wedding the next month. She laughed at family stories and smiled next to her mother as the photographer snapped picture after picture. But then Logan waved her over and she disappeared with him onto the dance floor.

Cecile pulled out a spindly gold chair and sat next to her sister, watching a stream of well-wishers approach to offer Monique congratulations on her daughter's nuptials.

"This day must feel bittersweet," Cecile said.

"Well, you know what they say. I'm not losing a daughter, I'm gaining a son."

Julia was moving halfway across the country after the wedding. That sounded very much like losing a daughter to Cecile.

"It looks like your daughter may be next," Monique said, gesturing to where Logan was spinning Esme around on the dance floor. "She's really come into her own lately. So much more confident."

Confident wasn't the word Cecile would use. Controlled, maybe. "I can't put my finger on it," Cecile said, "but I think there's something wrong in their relationship."

Her sister frowned. "I haven't gotten that impression. Has she said anything?"

"No, but a mother knows these things."

Monique fiddled with her corsage. "It can be hard to let go, sometimes, when it comes to our kids." It was the same thing she had tried to tell Cecile about sleepaway camp and out-of-state college.

Cecile turned away. "Julia looks great in your dress," she said.

Her sister beamed. "I'm so happy she wanted to wear it."

How had not wearing it ever been an option?

"It feels like just yesterday you and I were getting married, doesn't it?" Monique said.

Cecile had no fond memories of her wedding day. She had walked down the aisle and into a bad marriage. She knew now that she should have worried less about the table centerpieces and more about her ex-husband's flaws.

When another couple came up to congratulate the mother of the bride, Cecile seized the opportunity to slip away. She scanned the room for Esme, eventually spying her deep in conversation with one of her older cousins. With Logan nowhere in sight, Cecile made a beeline for their table.

As she approached, she strained to hear what the other woman was saying that had Esme listening so intently. "Sometimes," the cousin said, "the only solution to an unhealthy relationship is to leave it behind." Cecile caught her breath. Finally, someone else seemed to understand that Esme was in the wrong situation.

Esme shook her head. "It's hard when it's your mother. But it's like she doesn't want me to be happy."

Shock rooted Cecile to her spot, then a wave of disbelief washed over her and sent her rushing away. She ran straight into Logan, who was approaching the table clutching three glasses of champagne.

"Having a nice time?" he said.

She glared at him. What was it about this man that made her daughter choose him over her? And how could she make him disappear before it was too late? She pushed past him, deaf to the sound of glasses crashing to the floor.

Cecile spent the rest of the wedding on her phone. It turned out hiring a hitman involved the dark web and sums of money she didn't have. Poisons were more accessible, but without her keys to Esme's house she would have trouble accessing Logan's food, and there was no guarantee she wouldn't poison Esme by mistake now that she ate the same odd things. She could try to tamper with his mountain bike, but from her observations he checked it over every time he rode it. And what if he suddenly decided Esme needed to start riding it too? When the bride and groom departed in a shower of confetti she was no closer to a plausible scheme.

Back at home, Cecile sat in Esme's room late into the night. She finally gave up on sleep and decided to unpack the china figurines she had tried to share with her daughter. She pulled out the shepherdess, then unwrapped a songbird on a branch. As she ran her finger along its porcelain feathers, a plan began to form. It was drastic, but she would do anything for Esme, especially when Esme wouldn't do it for herself.

The next morning, Celeste pulled up the picture she had taken of

Logan's training schedule. On the following Sunday he was going for a solo ride on Devil's Peak. A fortuitous choice, because the trail map she consulted online showed a point at which riders were forced to travel along a public road as they transitioned between two different sections of the trail.

Cecile pulled into a lay-by halfway up the peak a week later and stepped out of her car. She slung her binoculars around her neck and made sure the bird guide she had stuffed in her back pocket was clearly visible. Anyone passing by would think she had stopped to search among the branches for a titmouse or a towhee.

Scanning the hill above, she confirmed that the road was empty of other cars. When Logan emerged from the trees she jumped behind her own wheel and started the engine. As he came speeding around the curve Cecile hit the gas and aimed straight for him, but he saw her coming and stood on his brakes. She swerved to try and sideswipe him but missed, then overcorrected and careened across the road, through the railing, and over the edge of the drop-off. The last thing she saw was the shock of recognition on his face.

A steady beep guided Cecile back to consciousness. She opened the eye not swathed in gauze and took in her surroundings. Her elevated leg was encased in a cast, and bruises decorated her arms. Tubes and wires ran from both sides of her body to multiple machines.

She turned her head and gasped at the pain, then gasped even louder at the sight of Logan sitting in the bedside chair. Cecile's heart pounded wildly as her hand groped through her bedding for a nurse call button. Her one good eye searched frantically for things he could use to harm her.

"How are you doing?" Logan said. "You really should be dead now."

Was he threatening her? She thought of Esme, and how she could have died, or could still die, without a chance to say good-bye, or to tell her how much she loved her, or to say she was sorry.

"I could have left you there when your car went over, you know," Logan continued. "I mean, that was your plan for me, wasn't it? Instead,

I called 911 and waited until they rescued you."

Cecile opened her mouth but didn't say anything. She flinched as Logan hitched his chair closer.

"Guardrails saved you, Cecile. You couldn't stop yourself and they slowed you down. And Esme needed to put up some guardrails around your relationship to save herself. Do you think you can live with them?"

Cecile nodded tentatively, unsure what more he was going to demand given his knowledge of what she had done.

"Good," Logan said, "because I care more about your daughter than I do about getting even. Esme doesn't deserve to know that her mother was willing to attempt murder. So, as long as you promise to get some psychotherapy along with all the physical therapy you're going to need, I'll keep quiet. Do we have a deal?"

Cecile had been so in despair over Logan, but now he was offering her a way to avoid both prison and a life without Esme.

He picked up a bakery box and flipped it open. "I brought you some quinoa and date sugar cookies from the vegan bakery." He held the box out to her.

Cecile looked at the cookies, then at the guy who loved her daughter, and took what he was offering.

I Know
(Dionne Farris)
Columbia CBS Inc 1995

I Know is a song by American R&B singer Dionne Farris. Written by Milton Davis and William DuVall, it was released in January 1995 by Columbia Records as the first single from Farris' debut album, *Wild Seed – Wild Flower* (1994). The song was a hit in Farris's native United States, peaking at #4 on the Billboard Hot 100 and spending 10 consecutive weeks at #1on the Billboard Top 40/Mainstream chart, becoming that ranking's most successful song of 1995.

I Know
(What You Did in Pittsburgh)

A Vermont Radio Mystery
Nikki Knight

The best thing about owning a radio station is I get to play whatever I want. One day last foliage season, that's how I stopped a killer.

Let me spin the song that did it, Dionne Farris's marvelous one-hit wonder "I Know," and check my commercial log, and I'll tell you how I ended up adding amateur sleuth to my portfolio of nighttime jock, morning news chick, program director—and oh, yeah, full-time mom. Again.

The Simpson Foliage Fest, in mid-October, is the one weekend of the year our tiny Vermont town becomes a tourist destination, drawing folks from all over the country and the world. I suppose I shouldn't have been surprised to see Ted Haines and his latest wife. And finding me at the little WSV remote table when he walked into the high school gym had to be a sweet moment for Ted, who'd never made it out of Pittsburgh.

Serves the uppity hillbilly right, landing back the backwater after that big New York career, he probably thought.

Someone like Ted, a rabblerousing talk-show host with a huge voice and shriveled soul, would never understand why I'd chosen to come back to the place where I had my first on-air job. Unless he could see it as a failure.

Which, yes, that's how it started. A year in, though, it was proving to be not just the right choice, but a success for me, and the thousands of people in and around Simpson who were very glad to have their own local radio station again.

No, it wasn't the millions who'd once listened to *Jaye Jordan's Light Rock at Work* on Bright 105, the top adult contemporary station in New York. But it was good, important work, and had long since become far more than the port in a personal and professional storm.

The short version: just about the time my husband survived cancer and decided he wanted different things, mostly blonde and bodacious, Bright 105's owners decided to go sports talk. I took my buyout and my broken heart and bought WSV, the tiny station where I'd had my first on-air job 20 years ago, because the old owner was offering a deal—and my ex could get a job and live with his parents in the next town over.

Close enough for our tween daughter, far apart enough for us.

Better, the old morning man, my former boss, Rob Archer, was still in town, running a restaurant next door and raising a son with his husband, an assistant District Attorney. Rob, a radio lifer at heart, was willing to revive the morning show for a share of ad revenues. His son and my daughter quickly became besties. Plus, I reconnected with an old crush, which is a long (and happy) story for another day.

By the time our second Foliage Fest arrived, we weren't just surviving. We were thriving.

Ted wasn't, not that I thought of him often.

He'd been in the middle of a nasty divorce when we were both on staff at the Edison Radio flagship in Pittsburgh, years before I made it to New York, and through the radio grapevine I'd heard he was stalled because he was too angry for the syndicated talk world.

Quite an achievement, considering what's out there.

When I bought WSV and flipped the format from right-wing satellite talk to music and local public-interest last year, an old radio pal in Pittsburgh had offered to send me Ted, joking that even the Burgh's large audience of cranky white males was getting sick of him.

At the time, I hadn't been especially interested in the details, just laughing it off, since she and I had both brushed up against Ted's problem dealing with women as fellow professionals. Or adult humans.

The conversation came back to me, though, when I saw Ted and a small, very blonde woman who had to be twenty years his junior walking into the Simpson High School gym. He was still a large presence, literally and figuratively, an inch or so shorter than my six feet, but with a big frame and maybe thirty extra pounds, slouching in the rumpled khakis and expensive brown suede barn jacket of a slumming star. The woman was clearly doing her best to spend his money, wearing a buttery metallic-leather moto jacket, knit silk t-shirt, and jeans with a label I'd seen only in fashion magazines, never in person. Not to mention highlights and no-makeup-makeup that probably cost more than my monthly food budget.

As he passed the Simpson Police Drug Prevention Program booth, Ted made a big show of shaking hands with the middle-aged desk sergeant who was watching the fort, doing the whole buddy-buddy thing. When a very tall Black man in a leather trench cut into the conversation, Ted startled, then forced an aggressively friendly smile when Chief George Orr introduced himself.

Bet I'd hear about that later—Chief George's wife Alicia is a friend.

Ted's little trophy wife fluffed her hair, inspected her acrylic nails and looked bored.

"Looks like the rich flatlanders have arrived," Rob said, nodding to them as he took off his headset mic. He'd just done the top-of-hour setup for two p-m and started the music set.

In the traditional fashion of small local stations everywhere, Rob and I were spending the weekend at the remote booth, going live open to close, spinning lots of up-tempo pop and oldies, and of course, taking requests.

"Not just any rich flatlanders," I said. "Ted Haines. Talk-show host I knew in Pittsburgh."

"Should I know his name?"

"Nah. But he'll think you should."

"Really? One of those, uh?"

"*So* one of those, believe me."

Ted turned for the booth just then. I saw the triumphant smile as he saw the sign with my name and Rob's, and his eyes flick to me. Saw the triumph fade a little as he realized the slim, polished woman at the booth wasn't the pudgy, scruffy recent college grad he'd known at Edison Pittsburgh.

Felt my stomach turn as his gaze warmed and I realized what he was thinking.

Scanned the booths to make sure my daughter and Rob's son were far away. We'd turned Ryan and Xavi loose with a generous budget for treats and tchotchkes, with the full expectation that we'd catch only the occasional glimpse of them until the end of the day, when they'd appear at the remote booth, tired, broke, and coming off a sugar high.

Especially good right now, because I couldn't guarantee I would keep my conversation with Ted appropriate for children—or air.

"Well, if it's not Jaye Jordan!" he roared, in a tone probably intended to be jovial, but closer to auditory assault.

Rob winced, cut his eyes to me.

"Hi, Ted," I said, flipping my mic up and slipping the headset off one ear so I could talk. "Fancy seeing you here."

"Well, the little woman wanted to do some leaf-peeping." He nodded to the wife, who was indeed literally little: probably a size zero and maybe five-two. Close to a foot shorter than me, anyhow.

"You're in the right place." I managed to smile at her, and she beamed vacuously back at me. I'd seen jellyfish with more original thoughts.

"Speaking of the right place," Ted said, "some change of pace for you, huh?"

"In the best possible way," I assured him sweetly. "I'd always wanted to own a station, and WSV was available."

"And you can't beat someone with New York expertise, you know." Rob added.

Ted's face went dark red as Rob's guess hit home. Pittsburgh was as far as he was going to go, and he knew it. "But nobody leaves New York once they make it."

"Unless they want to."

"Or get blown out for sports talk, am I right?" Ted finished with a guffaw. The classic conservative bro thing: I'm being funny and it's your fault if you're offended.

Rob scowled.

The wife tried to crease her brow in confusion and the Botox stopped her. "Well, Big Teddy, maybe they can tell us some nice places to go."

Oh, I'd like to tell Big Teddy where to go.

"Maybe you and your husband could meet us for dinner at that nice restaurant in the center of town," Ted said. "It doesn't look like much, but it's probably-"

"It's my place and it's the highest-rated casual dining restaurant in Windsor County." Rob's icy tone was a slap.

"Of course," Ted said, "you never know here in the back country. So—couples' night, Jaye?"

He had to know.

On the Edison Radio grapevine, the unraveling of my marriage was every bit as much public knowledge as the ignominious end of Bright 105. So, Ted was just being a schmuck.

His default setting.

"No, Ted," I said. "My husband and I split a year and a half ago. And my partner is busy tonight. But thank you for the thought." I didn't usually bring up my new fella for any number of good reasons, but Ted annoyed me enough that I wanted him to know I'd moved on.

"Well, it's good seeing you, Jaye. Surprised you're happy slumming here, but you look pretty good."

"I'm sorry," I said, moving on as I flatly refused to engage. "I don't think I've met your wife."

Because she was in sixth grade when we worked together in Pittsburgh.

"Oh, of course." He swept his arms like a spokesmodel and presented her. "Meet the former Jessica Dana, Miss Florida Guava, and current Mrs. Haines."

"Hi." She formed the single syllable as a pout, with her glossy nude lips and studied me with big, exceedingly blue eyes.

Color contacts have improved a lot. I could only tell at the very edge of the iris.

I held out a hand to shake, and she didn't take it. She was already diverted by the next booth.

"Oooh, look, Big Teddy! Beeswax and lavender body butter. I have to get some!"

The former Miss Guava teetered off on her spike-heeled boots, drawn to the beauty products as if by tractor beam.

Big Teddy chuckled. "She's easily distracted."

"No doubt." I carefully did not look at Rob, who was trying desperately not to laugh. "Well, I'm glad to see you happy. If I remember, you had some tough times back in the day."

"Rough few years until I met Jessica. She's a rare woman."

Definitely not well-done, anyhow, I thought as I looked at the clock on my CD. "Oh, jeez. We've got a break coming up. Come by and say hello before you leave, okay?"

"I get it. Duty calls."

With a rictus of a genial smile, he turned for the beeswax booth.

And there it might have ended, if I hadn't seen the expression on his face as Jessica, now lit-up and flirty, sniffed the various lip balms offered by our friendly—and surprisingly hot—neighborhood beekeeper.

"She'll have one of everything," Ted snapped. "Wrap it up."

Jessica's happy mask dropped for just an instant as he grabbed her wrist. Briefly, and probably not hard enough to leave a mark, but he got the message across.

I got a message too: Ted wasn't just a schmuck. He was much worse than that.

Time to get a little help from the Burgh.

Once I got my next music sweep set up, I rummaged through my contacts and found the phone number for my old radio pal: Alison Mrzawzy had been the overnight producer when I was the overnight editor in the newsroom. We were about the same age, but she'd always been sure she wanted to be a manager, just as I'd always known I wanted to be on the air.

We'd stayed pals, never competing for the same things in our crazy world, but occasionally able to offer support or insight. Alison, who was now running the whole RadioChannel cluster in Pittsburgh, had been the first to call and congratulate me the day the trades ran word of my purchase of WSV. Her joke about Ted had been nothing but a teasing callback to our misspent youth.

It wasn't now.

"Hey, Jaye!" She picked right up. "Thank you for giving me an excuse to leave the PTA Book Fair."

"Oh, jeez. I'm sorry-"

"Honey, I'd come up there and tech your remote if I thought I could get away with it. There is nothing worse than trying to produce an event in the middle of petty drama."

"They dragged you into chairing, didn't they?" I asked. I'd been through a similar disaster at Ryan's elementary school.

"They did. Fool that I am, I figured it would be easy and they'd do what I tell them." She sighed. "Managing these women's egos is worse than the talk show hosts."

Since several of her Pittsburgh hosts were nationally syndicated, she was really saying something. Also giving me an opening. "Speaking of talk show hosts, guess who's up here for Foliage Fest?"

"Oh, God. Tell me Zippy the Dude isn't drunk on the hayride."

"No, as far as I know, he's still your problem." Zippy Ronan, a classic dude-bro type whose main shtick was complaining about the women who had the misfortune to be in his life, was Allison's biggest money-maker and the bane of her existence.

"Well, that's something. So, who is there?"

"Ted Haines."

"Ugh. Still a nasty piece of work. He's only pulling in the angry grandpas now, you know. Edison would love to get rid of him, but they're terrified of the backlash."

"Thought maybe," I said as she confirmed my suspicions about Ted's career. Now to get some help with the rest. "He must be bringing it in on endorsements or something because wife number two is spending plenty on clothes and such."

"Wife number two?" Alison asked.

"Well, he was in the middle of that divorce when we worked with him, so I just assumed she was the new hire."

"Newer than you think. She's wife number three."

"Ow. Two divorces," I said. One had been more than enough for me. I felt sorry for Ted.

"No. Second one died. Some kind of OD, I think."

"Ugh."

"Yeah. I don't remember all the details, just that they were starting divorce proceedings and the timing was awfully convenient."

The suggestion was even more evil than I'd thought of Ted. "Are you thinking…"

"I'm not thinking anything that could get either of us sued," Alison said her tone careful and clear. "But it's Pittsburgh, and he's a very public friend to the police, so is it possible that people didn't look as closely as they might?"

"Ah," I said, keeping my tone as neutral as hers.

"Yeah. Tread carefully around this SOB, Jaye. He doesn't seem to see women as human."

"I WANT *WHO WAS QUEEN ELIZABETH!*"

The off-speaker cry reminded me Alison was in the middle of her PTA book fair.

"Yikes! Talk later," I said.

"Sorry. I have to go put out a fire."

"Only if you torch the mom."

"Don't give me ideas, Jaye."

Alison had given me plenty of ideas, though.

Not that I had time to think about them.

Over at the booth, Rob was finishing his last break and firing a song. Time for me to spell him while he wandered the booths with Xavi and Tim. I waved him off with the commercial log and started organizing the next couple of hours.

After the first break, I talked up a pair of anniversary requests that had come in over the last hour and checked off the spots on the log. As I finished signing the current page, I looked up and saw Jessica Haines inspecting the gorgeous sunset ombre glass pieces at the artisan across the aisle. Bellows Falls Glassworks wasn't as well-known as Simon Pearce up in Windsor, but their stuff was spectacular and insanely expensive.

Jessica was buying the biggest thing in the booth, a martini set complete with pitcher, six glasses, and stirrer stick. I could probably afford the stick.

After the glassmaker wrapped up her four-figure purchase in lovely splotchy tissue paper and gently stacked them in an artfully printed brown paper bag, Jessica turned to me.

"How do you not buy everything?" she asked in her chirpy tone, with a fake little grin.

"Most of it's out of my price range," I admitted. "But I love events like this when I get to look at it."

"Aw, c'mon, you have to be doing okay. You own the radio station."

Oh, to be young and naïve.

"Um, yeah." I kept a carefully neutral tone. I wanted to draw her in, not scare her silly. "How are you enjoying the trip?"

"Oh, it's wonderful." She beamed. "The leaves are so pretty, and everything is so cute."

"Cute." I nodded. How was I going to introduce the topic? *How about those Steelers? Hey, do you feel safe at home?* Or maybe: *Planning to try the applejack? Don't take a cup from your husband.*

"Cows and sheep—and we saw llamas in a field yesterday, too."

"Nice." Oh, the hell with it. "Look, I worked with Ted back in the day, and I know some things about him."

Her eyes widened enough that I worried her color contacts might slip. "Ted? Really?"

"Really. Do you know what happened to his wife?"

"Oh, she had a problem." Studied sad face as she leaned in with a whisper. "Opioids, you know."

"They seem to be everywhere," I agreed. "But she-"

"Are you suggesting that he—that I…"

"I'm suggesting you may want to keep an eye to your safety. That's all."

"Well, that's a horrible thing to say!" Jessica huffed. "How dare you?"

"Couldn't live with myself if I didn't warn you," I said simply.

"Well, there's nothing to warn me about." She tossed her head at me with a sniff. "I don't have to listen to this."

"No. But you might do well to think about it."

"I don't think so!"

Well, I tried.

As Jessica stormed off, the red soles of her boots flashing as she minced down the aisle, I segued into the next song and reached for my phone. Maybe I could find some background that would help.

It took all of a minute.

Wife number two wasn't the only woman to leave Ted Haines' life in a body bag. The ex had died in a fall down the basement stairs at the home she'd gotten in the divorce. Found at the bottom of the flight, roughly a week after her death, when she didn't show up to pick up the kids from summer camp.

Pittsburgh police guessed at the time of death because Ted was apparently the last person to see her when she handed the kids over to him for the drive up to Camp Loch Haven.

Adding times may be my best math skill, but it's not my only one.

Ted's wives added up to one very damning solution, whether Jessica wanted to believe it or not.

But how the hell to flush him out?

Well, I still had a show to do. Let it cook for a few minutes while I set up the next music sweep. And as I looked through the remote kit, I found the perfect song—and a plan. Every once in a while, an encyclopedic knowledge of midrange pop music comes in very handy.

With a little help from Miss Dionne Farris and just the right dedication, I might be able to provoke Ted into incriminating himself. I scanned the scene, looking to be sure our self-important visitor was within earshot. He was at the applejack booth near the entrance again, with Jessica.

That'll work.

Carefully pulling the CD out of the jewel box, I kept an eye on Ted as I put it in the player and loaded a couple more songs so I'd be free to deal with…whatever happened.

Then I straightened my headset mic and clicked it on, talking over the music intro.

Showtime.

"You're listening to WSV Radio live at the Foliage Festival. Come on over and say hi—and if you've got a request, I'll be happy to play it. In the meantime, here's one for an old friend from Pittsburgh. Ted Haines, my man, you'll know exactly what this means…"

And the wise, smooth voice began: *"I know…"*

My plan would have worked perfectly, except that I got a text from Ryan:

Ma, I need my sweater.

Since my Wrangler, with Ryan's sweater in the back, was just outside the back door, one booth over, I figured I could scoot out, grab it and skip back within less than a minute. Tim, Rob's husband, was passing by, and I grabbed his arm.

"Hold the fort a sec, okay?"

Tim, no stranger to battlefield promotions during remotes, slipped into the booth. "Will you need me to fire the next song?"

"Nah. I'm just getting something from the car. It'll be thirty seconds."

Famous last words.

Outside, it was cold, and mostly dark, with the waning sun and the shadow of the school building. A chill crept up my back.

I told myself it was the weather, and not Scotch-Irish radar.

Grabbed Ryan's sweater, the poison green she favored practically glowing in the low light. As she got older, she was being drawn to more normal colors, but she still couldn't quite resist the blinding shades.

Maybe I needed to start steering her style a little.

"What the hell do you think you're doing?"

Ted was between me and the door.

He looked like he had some applejack under his belt. I'm not a small woman, but I always remember my self-defense instructor's warning: if it comes to a physical fight, you've already lost.

But I had a secret weapon. My wireless headphone mic was still connected, even if it wasn't in place. Betting Ted wouldn't know what I was doing, I fidgeted with my jacket and turned on the mic.

"What the hell were you saying to my wife?"

"Told her she might want to watch her back, considering what happened to the last two."

Even in the moody late-afternoon light, I could see his face turn red. "What?"

"You may have had enough pull to put it past the Pittsburgh cops, but even now, I have a hard time believing anyone is unlucky enough to have two wives die suspiciously in five years."

"What do you know about it?"

"I know, as the song says, enough. Your ex, dead at the bottom of the stairs, conveniently just when the kids left for summer camp. Did you throw her down while the kids were in the car, or take care of it on the way back?"

"I did nothing of the kind."

"Yeah, right." I held his gaze. "What about your second wife? The one who OD'd right after she started divorce proceedings?"

"Coincidence." He snapped each syllable like a projectile.

"Sure, Ted." I allowed my voice to drip with absolute contempt as I looked down at him. "It's just a coincidence that women who annoy you keep ending up dead."

"Shut up, Jaye. You don't know anything."

"Like I said, I know enough. And any decent investigation will turn up the rest."

"Screw you, Jaye. You don't get to ruin my life because yours didn't turn out."

"My life is just fine. And I didn't have to kill anybody to get it."

Ted huffed, puffing up like an angry reptile. "You're a nobody. You always were, and you always will be."

Whew. I thought he'd never get mad. This wasn't where and how I wanted to have the confrontation, but it would do. Time to send him over.

"I was never nobody, Ted. And you were never much of a person." I dropped my gaze below his belt. "Or much else."

It had the desired—excuse the repulsive reference—effect.

Ted went for me.

My old martial arts instructor was wrong this time.

Because what Ted said, and everyone at the Foliage Festival, and within range of our small, but quite powerful transmitter, heard, made him the loser:

"I should kill you too."

Before he could get his hands on me, I got mine up—and landed a knee where it would do the most good. He let out a high-pitched wail and crumpled.

"I'll get you, you bitch!" he hissed as he writhed on the ground.

"You've got a few other things to worry about right now, Mr. Haines," Chief George said, as he walked out the gym door, trailed by a very anxious Rob.

Ted, who was still having trouble breathing, glared up at the Chief.

The only thing worse than being bested by a girl was being turned over to a Black police chief. From the tiny wry smile trying to break through Chief George's game face as he dragged Ted to his feet, I could tell he knew it, too.

"I want a lawyer."

"Probably a good choice," Tim said, walking out onto the pavement. He turned to Rob with a small sigh, as his demeanor changed from amiable husband to prosecutor on duty. "Looks like I'm going to miss dinner while I write up the arrest affidavit."

"I'll live." Rob smiled. "We'll save you some apple pie."

"Dutch, please. I like the crumb topping."

"Oh, so do we," Chief George said, as he clicked the last cuff. "Alicia bought one of those Macoun pies from Drude's Orchard."

"Nothing better," Rob agreed.

"The mile-high is pretty good with cinnamon ice cream," I said.

"You could put cinnamon ice cream on crumb-top and have the best of both worlds." Tim suggested.

"Too much?" Rob asked.

"A little." The Chief considered for a moment. "In a good way."

"What is *wrong* with you people?" Ted howled. Turned out there was something even more humiliating than his apprehension: being ignored.

"Nothing, Mr. Haines," Chief George said, as he steered Ted into the door. "Not one damn thing."

Applause broke out as we walked in the door. There were a few "Yay, Jaye's" from my female friends, and whistles from the cops and firefighters for Chief George. Ryan and Xavi raised their maple cotton candy to us in a very tween salute.

Ted cringed a little.

"Oh, don't worry," Chief George said, his tone dry and cool. "It gets worse from here."

Everyone close enough to hear the chief's calm tone quieted down and waited.

I suddenly realized Jessica was nowhere in sight. And she should have been. Should have been running up to Ted, weeping and swearing it wasn't so.

Where was she?

"Gonna be a nice couple night in the lockup," said Chief George.

"What?" Ted gasped.

I stared.

"Not sure if you knew this, Mr. Haines, but Jessica Dana isn't your wife's real name."

Ted's jaw dropped open.

"You're pretty lucky. She looked familiar to me, and I did an image search. Turns out the cops in Florida had put out a BOL. She's a real black widow. Best we can tell, she's poisoned at least three husbands, two fatally, under different names."

Well, none of us had that on our bingo cards.

Chief George sent me an eyebrow and a tiny smile as he walked Ted to the exit.

"Don't forget the pie," Tim said, patting Rob's arm on his way.

Show over. Most of the crowd returned to cider and jam and crafts. Ryan walked over to the booth and handed me a cotton candy and grudgingly accepted a hug from her boring mom. Neither of us would admit it, but we'd really needed it.

As she scampered off with Xavi, Rob elbowed me. "Good day's work, partner."

I pulled my headset back into place. "Oh, we're not done yet. Let's get back to the remote."

"What do you want to play?"

"Anything but a one-hit wonder."

Sunny Came Home
(Shawn Colvin)
Columbia 1997

Sunny Came Home is a folk-rock song by American musician Shawn Colvin. It is the opening track on her 1996 concept album, *A Few Small Repairs*, and was sent to Top 40 radio in the US on February 4, 1997, followed by a release as a CD and cassette single later that year. In the United Kingdom, the song was released in July 1997 but did not chart until a re-release in May 1998.

Sonny Came Home

Adam Meyer

Colvin, Tennessee—October 2005

After being on the go for almost three hours, I finally stood still, closing my eyes, dreaming of being on a tropical island. For a moment I was there—palm trees swaying, water lapping against sand, cool drink in my hand—and then real life cut in.

"Hey lady, can we get some more sodas or what?"

I plastered on a smile and headed for table six. A bunch of high school kids who'd ordered barely any food and wanted endless drink refills. Had me and my friends been this obnoxious back in the day? Sadly, I knew the answer.

As I turned from table six, I saw movement out the front window. Someone on the sidewalk near the hardware store, beneath the streetlight. A woman about my age, long hair hanging in her face. If I didn't know better, I would've thought …

No, it can't be her. Sunny's gone and she's never coming back.

Was that true?

Everyone in town thought so, including me. Or at least, I'd told myself I believed it. And wasn't that the same thing?

I forced myself to focus on my work. Table four still had to order, table eight wanted dessert, table ten had gotten a burger with cheese instead of plain. But I kept glancing out the plate glass window.

What if it really is Sunny?

Even if my old friend had come back, I knew one thing for sure: I was just about the last person Sunny would want to see.

During the next hour, I returned to table four for another round of refills. Coke and Dr. Pepper for the boys, Diet Cokes for the girls. Same as in my day. Sure, the fashions were different—baggy jeans and Air Jordans instead of flannel and combat boots—but not much else had changed.

As the kids were scraping together money for their tab, a boy in a black sweatshirt asked me if I had change for a twenty. I went to the register, counting out a ten and some singles. The boy watched closely.

"Hey, you're Julie Tassano, right?"

I nodded wearily.

"You went to high school with my brother Troy, right? Troy Taylor."

I tried to picture Troy and couldn't, but then the image came. A boy who'd warmed the bench on the baseball team, not the best student in our class but not the worst, either.

"Yeah, I remember him. Class of '96. What's he up to now?"

"He lives in Nashville, he's got a really cool apartment downtown, and sometimes when I visit he takes me to bars with him." He took the bills I held out. "Thanks for the change."

The boy went back to his friends. I stood there, smile melting. How had Troy Taylor managed to escape Colvin and yet here I was, working the same job I'd picked up my senior year of high school. A gig I'd expected to ditch as soon as I headed off to Vanderbilt, only my mom had gotten cancer and I was the only one around to take her to doctor's appointments.

By the time my mother passed, four endless years later, all my friends had already finished college and I'd been out of school so long that going back seemed impossible. I didn't love being a waitress but I could do it for another six months, at least until I figured out my next move. Only now I was twenty-seven and still here.

I watched the teenagers file out and went to clean up their table. They'd left a thick wad of bills, but when I counted them, the tip was only three dollars and twenty-four cents. I pocketed the money with a sigh.

Twenty minutes later, I waved goodnight to my coworkers and headed out of the diner. The house I'd inherited from my mother was only a mile or so up the road. Even though my shifts usually left me wiped, I liked to walk. The fresh air felt good, especially on a crisp fall night like this.

I was halfway down the block, hands in the pockets of my fleece coat, when I heard footsteps behind me. Likely one of my coworkers. Had I forgotten to clock out?

I turned and saw someone approaching. Long hair, denim jacket.

My breath caught. I looked at Sunny, her face half in shadow, a streetlight catching the glint in her eyes. Nine years had passed, but somehow she hadn't aged a day.

"What're you doing here?" I asked, caught between surprise and disbelief. "I didn't think …."

"Let's go, Jules," Sunny said, grabbing my arm. "I need you to come with me."

"Sunny, I—"

My eyes went to Sunny's face. I looked for a hint of a smile, some sign she was kidding. But Sunny had always been a serious person.

"What's going on?" I asked. "Why are you here?"

"You'll see. Now come on."

Sunny tugged on my arm, leading me away from the diner. All through high school, I had followed my then-best friend everywhere, and though it had been nine years, not much had changed. I would've gone wherever Sunny led.

As we headed down the sidewalk, I glanced over, not quite believing. For years, I had wondered what it would be like if I ever got to talk to Sunny again. I'd thought of all the things I might say.

Where've you been?

Why'd you stay away so long?

I'm sorry.

Now that the moment was here, however, nothing I'd imagined

saying seemed quite right. Instead, I felt a crackle of excitement, the way I used to whenever I went out with Sunny, even if it was just to the Colvin Mall or the Vermillion Theater.

"Get in," Sunny said. "You drive."

Sunny had stopped next to an old minivan. I looked at it in surprise.

"This is yours?"

"I said get in. Let's go."

I got in on the driver's side. The overhead light didn't come on. In the back seat was a pile of blankets, boxes stacked up beside them. More junk was piled in the back, blocking my view through the rear window. The key was in the ignition and I turned it, then looked over as Sunny slid in.

"Where're we going?" I asked, turning on the headlights.

"Jimmy Berkley's house. On Seeger Road. He still lives there, doesn't he?"

"You don't want to go there."

"No offense, Jules, but how the hell do you know what I want?"

I took the point. But even though Sunny and I hadn't been friends in a long time, I knew this would be a mistake. "I just … maybe we should …"

Sunny pointed at the windshield. "Take us there."

The minivan jerked as we pulled away from the curb. I stared out the smudged windshield at the gray swath of street ahead. In the rearview, the pile of blankets shifted. I nearly jumped in surprise.

"You okay back there, Harper?" Sunny said.

A little girl, camouflaged by blankets, murmured something and drifted off again.

"That's my daughter." Sunny stared out as old storefronts gave way to clapboard houses. "She's eight."

I didn't say anything. Like Sunny, math had never been my favorite subject but I knew what the girl's age meant.

"So Sunny, where do you live these days?" I tried to keep my tone light, but I was aware of the little girl and where we were headed.

"We've been all over, really. For the last couple months we've been living right here."

At first I didn't get it. Here in Colvin? How could Sunny be back in town that long without word getting out? But then I glanced at the pile of stuff in the rearview and understood. Sunny and her daughter had been living in the minivan.

"So, I'm guessing you never left," Sunny said.

"Yeah." I pushed the word past a lump in my throat. "Not yet."

"It's funny, don't you think? I'm the one who wanted to stay and you always wanted to go, and then it turned out the opposite."

I gripped the wheel tightly, rounding the corner onto Seeger Road. Hadn't so much of my life been like that? Everything turning out backwards from how I thought it would. It hardly seemed remarkable anymore.

"We had some good times, didn't we?" Sunny asked.

"Yeah, of course."

I could still remember meeting Sunny on the first day of high school. My mom and I had just moved into Colvin from Greene County, and I hadn't known a single person in the vast cafeteria. Sunny had seen me looking around, lost, and waved me over. From that day on, we were fast friends. Eating lunch together, doing homework and watching *Charlie's Angels* reruns after school, then talking on the phone for hours more.

All I wanted was for things to go on like that forever. But then, at the start of senior year, we got Mr. Berkley for English and everything changed.

"Why are you doing this?" I asked.

"It's a short drive and a long story. It'll have to wait."

I shot Sunny a look. "What I mean is, why are you dragging me into this?"

"Because I need a witness."

I fell silent, letting those words tumble around. A witness. What did Sunny intend to do? And why did she want me to be there? Was this payback for how our friendship had ended? Or something else?

The shuffling of blankets from the backseat. A small, high-pitch voice asked: "Mama?"

"Yes, honey?" I heard something in Sunny's voice I didn't recognize, a mix of love and weariness and pride. "What is it?"

"Are we gonna stop soon?"

"Yes, Harper. We're gonna stop soon. Very soon."

The road curved up a slight hill, a small cluster of homes perched on top. I turned down a tree-lined street and onto a cul de sac, aiming for the house at the end. Two cars sat in the driveway, a Volvo station wagon and a sportscar. I parked behind them and looked over at Sunny.

"You sure you want to do this?"

Sunny said nothing at first and then turned around, reaching for something. "You stay here, okay? Mama will be right back."

I felt like she was moving in slow motion as I opened the car door and crossed the driveway. Sunny was beside me, a Dora the Explorer backpack slung over her shoulder. I tilted my head toward the house, the second story dark, light glowing from behind the white curtains that covered the big front window.

"What're you gonna say to him?" I asked, as Sunny and I approached the house together. We had fallen into a rhythm, side by side. Just like old times.

"I'm going to tell him the truth. And tell him it's time to give me what he owes me."

"And what's that?"

Sunny didn't say anything. She had turned back to the minivan, where her daughter—Harper—had pressed her face against the side window, peering out. Sunny blew her a kiss.

"Look, you haven't done anything wrong," Sunny said. "When it's over, you can just tell people I'm the one that made you come."

I felt something cold and slick unfurl in my belly. Of course I hadn't done anything wrong. And what did Sunny mean, when *what* was over? I was just trying to be there for Sunny, a witness, though I still had no idea what that meant. But I was starting to get some ideas.

"Don't." I reached for Sunny's arm but stopped short of touching her. "Let's just walk away."

"It's too late for that."

Sunny went up to the porch and slammed her palm against the front door. Again, and then again. The sound echoed in the still night.

Faintly a voice called out from inside the house. Sunny raised her hand again when a face appeared in the narrow strip of glass beside it. I had seen Mr. Berkley—Jimmy as he'd said to call him when I served him at the diner—several times since graduation, though not in several months.

"What the hell?"

Mr. Berkley—Jimmy—opened the door, his voice a loud whisper. He looked at me as if confused, then noticed Sunny. His expression changed, both surprised and angry at once. "Sunny, is that you?"

He stepped onto the porch, closing the door most of the way behind him.

"Hi, Jimmy."

He stared at Sunny. "You can't be here."

"Well, you wouldn't return my phone calls or answer my letters, so … I had to come. And I'm not leaving until we talk."

"Keep your voice down." He spoke in an angry whisper. "My wife's sound asleep upstairs. You're lucky you didn't wake her up already."

Sunny reached into the pocket of her denim jacket and looked at me. I said nothing. I'd told her not to do this but she wouldn't listen. When it came to Mr. Berkley—it's Jimmy, just call me Jimmy now—she never had.

"If you want to talk, I can meet you in the morning, before school." He looked at the houses nearby. "I can't have people thinking …"

Thinking what, that he'd get involved with one of his students? Sunny was a grown woman now. Besides, despite the rumors that swirled around him, so far as I knew his job teaching high school English had never been under serious threat. As people said, was it his fault if some of his students threw themselves at him? Besides, he was forty now and married, surely he'd changed his ways.

"This can't wait until the morning." Sunny pulled something dark and long out of her pocket. A gun. "I've waited long enough as it is."

"Is that a … Jesus, Sunny, what're you doing?"

"Let's go inside."

"But … I can't just …"

Sunny aimed the gun at his chest. Jimmy seemed shaken and so was I.

"Sunny, what're you doing?" I said, then turned to Jimmy. "I didn't know …"

Didn't know what? That she had a gun? That she was going to confront Jimmy Berkley? Maybe, but I knew Sunny was bound to do something dangerous. That was part of why I'd come in the first place.

"Let's go," Sunny said, pushing inside. Jimmy backed away, making room for her. I followed, closing the door behind us.

I'd never been in Jimmy Berkley's house before. I had met Sunny out front a few times, after their "study sessions." Whenever he invited me in, I made some excuse, as if crossing the threshold would make me an accomplice somehow.

"Like what you've done with the place," Sunny said, the gun at her side as she looked around the living room. I took in the oversized sofa, flat-screen TV and surround sound system, suggestions of a life far from the one Sunny and her daughter had in their minivan.

"Come on," Jimmy said softly.

He moved through a rounded doorway into the kitchen. Sunny sat at the table, setting the gun down on a yellow placemat. She leaned back and kicked her legs out in front of her like she had just been invited to stay for dinner.

"I used to feel so at home here," she said. "You remember how we'd hang out and you'd bring me an afterschool snack, like my dad or something? Only my father never did that kind of thing."

That was true. After school, Sunny's father was usually in his workshop, the sound of machinery going as he worked on the homemade furniture he sold in town. He never said much to Sunny, his only child, and what he did say was dismissive or mean. Sunny's mom had run away years earlier and cut off all contact with them. Her dad had never gotten over it.

"I'm all out of cookies, Sunny, and I'm almost out of patience too." Jimmy ran a hand through his thinning hair, looking older than his forty years. "Now let's get this over with. What do you want?"

Sunny looked around as if baffled not by where she was but by when. Living in Colvin for so long, I understood. Sometimes, it was easy to feel confused as to whether you were twenty-seven or seventeen.

"I need money," Sunny said. "I lost my job a few months ago and I've had trouble finding a new one."

"Money?" He nearly spat the word. "So, this is what, some kind of shakedown?"

Sunny shook her head. "All these years, I never asked for anything from you. Not a thing."

Jimmy began pacing around the kitchen. "Money … I'm a goddamn English teacher, I haven't got money … and besides, why would I give any to you?"

"To help support my daughter." Sunny took a deep breath. "Our daughter."

Jimmy huffed. "Is that why you're here? Because you've got some crazy idea in your head?"

"It's not an idea. It's the truth."

"It's a lie. I never …"

Sunny turned to me. "Tell him, Jules. You were there."

Now I saw why she had brought me, because I was the witness, the one who'd seen it all: the way their relationship progressed from after-school tutoring to her going to his house for private study sessions. But I said nothing, watching Sunny's hands on the table. Her fingers were still wrapped around the grip of the gun.

"You're being ridiculous," Jimmy said, sounding outraged. "I don't know who the father of your kid is but it's sure as hell not me."

Sunny's face darkened. "You're the only one it could've been."

His chair scraped on the hardwood as he backed away from the table. "Get out of my house. Right now."

"Sunny." I wished my voice was as steady as hers. "Maybe we should go."

She ignored me, angling the gun toward him. "Do you know how I felt when I found out I was pregnant? Scared, yes, but happy too. Because I thought we'd be together. I came over here to tell you the news but you weren't around so I just headed home. I went straight to my room, lay on my bed and made a list of baby names." She blinked, tears in her eyes. "But I always knew I wanted to call her Harper."

Jimmy was silent, staring blankly at Sunny. He didn't understand but I did. *To Kill a Mockingbird* was the first book we read in English class that year, and though it was a couple of months before Mr. Berkley started inviting Sunny to meet after school, she fell in love with him over those discussions of Scout and Atticus Finch. Of course, Sunny's little girl was named Harper.

"I left you a bunch of messages but you never called me back, so I didn't get to tell you the news until I got to school the next day." Sunny blinked away tears. "And then you … you were so mad, said I had to get rid of the baby. You told me we'd never be together, that it was just a stupid fantasy and I needed to grow up."

Sunny's tears flowed freely now. I started to cry a little myself. Because I remembered what came next, when Sunny waited for me outside chemistry class. She'd told me everything Mr. Berkley had said. And I said he was right, that at seventeen she was too young to be a mother. Sunny had stared at me in disbelief, but I kept going. He wasn't the one who said their relationship was just a stupid fantasy and she needed to grow up. That was me.

Sobbing, she had run off. When I went to her house later, she wouldn't answer. The next day, she didn't show up at school, either. I went to find her, but her father said she had run off. I waited for her to come home and she didn't. Not the next day or the next week or even the next month.

Later, I heard that Sunny had settled up north and had a baby.

A couple of years after she ran off, her dad left town too and a new family moved into their house.

I never heard from her again. And I didn't know if I ever would.

Turns out you were wrong.

"Sunny, I don't know what kind of stories you've been telling yourself …" Jimmy shook his head in disbelief. "I was friendly to you because you were a good student and lonely, but that's it." He looked at me. "Julie, I suggest you take Sunny home."

"He's right," I said, turning to Sunny. "We should go."

"Not yet." She raised the gun with her right hand, leveling it at his chest. "Not until he gives me what he owes me."

Jimmy stared at her, mouth open. "What're you … you're nuts …."

"Sunny, put that away." I forced myself to act calm, even as panic swept through me. "There's got to be a better way to deal with this."

"I've tried every other way. And I've got to take care of my daughter."

Jimmy put his hands up in surrender. "You want money? Fine, I can give you …" He pulled bills from his wallet, counting them out the way I did at the end of a shift. "… eight-six, ninety-six, a hundred and six dollars."

"It's not just the money. My daughter deserves to know who her father is."

"It's not me." He approached Sunny, standing in front of her now and waving the cash. "Here, just take it."

"I told you, I don't just want—"

Jimmy flung the bills at Sunny. Her hands went up instinctively to her face, him grabbing her right wrist. As I started to move toward them to referee, Sunny yelped. Jimmy had twisted her wrist back and loosened her hold on the gun. He snatched it by the barrel and took a step back, safely out of reach.

"Now enough is enough." Jimmy waved the gun at Sunny. "Get the hell out of my house."

A sound of creaking hardwood and then a shadow moving in the doorway. "Jimmy, what's going on?"

Turning, I saw a woman. She had a heart-shaped face and long blond hair like Sunny. Jimmy's wife, Tara, had come into the diner with him back when they were dating, though not since they got married. Her hands were set on her rounded belly. She looked to be about six months pregnant.

"Who're you?" She looked from me to Sunny. "And what're you doing in my house?"

Something inside Sunny seemed to crumble. She glanced at me as if to say, you should've told me. But hadn't I told her not to come?

"Jimmy, what's going on?" Tara asked.

He put the hand with the gun behind his back. "It's nothing."

Tara padded forward in fuzzy pink slippers. She didn't seem frightened, as if she believed that her husband would simply handle things. Did she sometimes still think of him as Mr. Berkley? After all, she'd been a couple years behind us in high school. Jimmy had told anyone who'd listen that they didn't get together until after she graduated, but did people really believe him? I didn't.

"It sure looks like something," Tara said.

"This is Sunny … she's a former student. Julie, too … they came to say hello, and they were just leaving …"

I turned to Sunny. "Come on. Let's go."

Sunny looked stricken. Things hadn't played out the way she wanted.

"We'll talk to Mr. Berkley—Jimmy—some other time," I said.

I led Sunny back into the living room. She dragged the Dora the Explorer backpack behind her, moving as though underwater.

"Jules, please." Her words were nearly engulfed by a sob. "I can't just give up like this."

"Let's talk about it outside."

I steered Sunny by the arm to the front door. When I looked back,

Jimmy was watching. He nodded at me, as if grateful, which made me feel like a traitor. I had meant to help Sunny, not him.

The night air was cool on my skin. I started to lead Sunny to the driveway but she planted herself on the front walk, looking up at the house, and reached into the backpack. I shifted my attention from her to the minivan, where the little girl had pressed her face to the glass, watching.

"C'mon, let's go. It must be past Harper's bedtime."

"I can't."

Sunny dropped the backpack, holding up something the size of an encyclopedia. It took me a moment to realize what it was. A gas can.

"Sunny, don't!"

She twisted off the cap and stomped back to the front porch, spilling gasoline as she went. I charged at her, but she spun around, splashing gas all over me too. I backed away, the sickly-sweet smell piercing my temples.

"You're making a mistake," I said. "If you want Jimmy to pay … take him to court, force him to get a paternity test. Just … don't do this."

Sunny dropped the gas can and pulled out a book of matches from her pocket. "He'll never admit he's the father. Never. He's got his own family, his own life. I'm nothing to him."

At the front window, Jimmy Berkley looked out. His eyes locked on Sunny, going wide when he saw the matches.

"Sunny, please." I backed up half a step, afraid of going up in flames, but not willing to abandon my friend again. Not yet. "Don't do anything you'll regret."

"I don't regret any of it." Sunny smiled, like she was a million miles way. "Not a single thing."

At the front door, Jimmy stepped out on the porch, Sunny's gun in his hands. He aimed it at her, arms steady. "What the hell're you doing, Sunny?"

If she heard him, she didn't show it, just stared at the matchbook in her hands.

I ignored him too. "You're a mother now, Sunny, and Harper needs you. I need you too. I deserved it, the way you left me behind, but I've missed you like hell … and I want a second chance. But first … you've got to walk away."

"I hate the way you treated me," she said, tearing out a match. Was she talking to Jimmy or me? "And a part of me still loves you, will maybe always love you. Is that fucked up or what?"

Jimmy moved out further onto the porch, sniffing, the gun aimed in front of him. "Sunny, get the hell out of here. Right now. Or I'll call the cops."

"And tell them what?" I asked. "How you got her pregnant when she was just seventeen? And how you've been sleeping with your students for years? I'm sure they'd love to hear all about it."

He glared at me. "You're a liar, just like Sunny. And you better watch what you say about me."

Behind him, his wife Tara appeared, whispering. He shook his head at her, arguing too softly for me to hear, the gun still out in front of him.

Ignoring them, I took a step toward Sunny, my stomach clenching. "Years ago, you came to me for help and I blew it. I'm sorry. I should've told someone about Mr. Berkley, the way he treated you, and … I should've stopped him from doing that to other girls. I made mistakes, we all have. But this isn't going to fix them."

Sunny said nothing and struck the match.

She stared into the tiny flame, and for a moment part of me wanted her to drop it, and let us all go up in a roaring blaze. But she didn't, and the fire ate at the match, burning down to her fingers, until she blew it out.

"I can't," she said, dropping the match.

"That's okay." I took Sunny by the arm, leading her away from the house. "You don't need to do anything."

When I looked back at the house, the door was closed. Tara watched us through the front window, hands on her rounded belly. Then she turned back, as if Jimmy had called out. A moment later she disappeared, pulling the white curtains shut behind her.

As Sunny and I crossed the lawn, the door of the minivan slid open. "Mama!"

The little girl, Harper, ran at full speed, blond hair streaming out behind her. She threw her arms around Sunny, holding tight. I saw now that the backpack Sunny held matched Harper's Dora the Explorer pajamas.

"It's okay, baby. You're okay. Mama's got you."

Sunny carried Harper into the rear of the minivan, where the girl curled up in the blankets again. I got in on the passenger side this time. Sunny sat behind the wheel. She smelled of gasoline and fear-sweat, but there was a light in her eyes, brighter than any flame.

"You know, I dreamed about it so many times," she said quietly. "The fire climbing the walls … the flames licking the night sky … and me watching from above, like an eagle, and feeling right, really *right*, for the first time in years."

I nodded. "Then why didn't you do it?"

"In the dreams, I was alone," she said, starting the engine.

I waited for her to say more but she didn't.

For a minute we rode in silence, angling down the hill back toward town, and then Sunny looked at me. "So what do I do now?"

"Let's go to my place," I said. "It's the same house where I lived with my mom … I could just never bring myself to sell it. There's plenty of extra room, so you and Harper can stay as long as you want, and one way or another we'll figure it out."

Sunny nodded wearily.

"You still know the way?" I asked.

It turned out she did.

Spinning the Hits

Steve Liskow (www.steveliskow.com) played bass in The Domino Cane Sugar Company & Travel Agency, which broke up after one gig because they couldn't fit the band's name on the bass drum. He has published sixteen novels and nearly seventy short stories, was the first two-time winner of the Black Orchid Novella Award and has shortlisted for the Edgar Award and the Shamus Award. He still plays guitar. Steve also appears in the White City Press anthology *Janie's Got a Gun: Crime Fiction Inspired by the Music of Aerosmith.*

Vicki Erwin has been in the publishing industry for more than thirty years in various capacities, including sales, book distribution and as the owner of a bookstore in St. Charles, Missouri. She is the author of more than thirty books in varied genres: picture books, middle-grade mysteries and novels, local histories and true crime. She has an MFA in writing popular fiction from Seton Hill University. Vicki also appears in the White City Press anthology *Yeet Me in St. Louis.*

Kaye George is the author of *Death in the Time of Ice*, the first of the People of the Wind series, which was nominated for an Agatha Award for Best Historical Novel. Kaye is also the author of four other mystery series available through White City Press. More than fifty of her short stories appear in magazines and anthologies. She lives in Knoxville TN, where she is the cofounder of Smoking Guns, the local Sisters in Crime chapter. She also reviews for Suspense Magazine and edits the *What's Your Process* column in Mysterical-E magazine.

Judy Penz Sheluk is a Past Chair of Crime Writers of Canada, a former journalist and magazine editor. She is also the multiple award-winning author of seven bestselling mystery novels, two books on publishing, and several short stories. She is also the editor/publisher of five Superior Shores Anthologies, including the 2025 Derringer- and Silver Falchion- nominated *Larceny & Last Chances*. Find her at www.judypenzsheluk.com

John M. Floyd is the author of more than a thousand short stories in publications like *AHMM, EQMM, Strand Magazine, The Saturday Evening Post, Best American Mystery Stories*, and *Best Mystery Stories of the Year*. A former Air Force captain and IBM systems engineer, John is also an Edgar nominee, a Shamus Award winner, a six-time Derringer Award winner, and a past recipient of the Edward D. Hoch Memorial Golden Derringer for lifetime achievement. One of his stories recently appeared in the White City Press anthology, *A Killing at the Copa*.

Linda Kay Hardie Linda Kay Hardie's varied careers ranged from radio disk jockey to adjunct college professor. That may help explain her story here, although she reluctantly admits it also could have been due to the Spanish Torrontes wine. Or maybe the cheap scotch she drinks to forget that she can't afford decent scotch.

Linda writes horror, crime, historical, and SF/fantasy stories and poetry, plus essays (often about cats but sometimes baseball). In 2022, she was honored with the Sierra Arts Foundation's Literary Arts Award for fiction in Reno, Nevada. That came only with a check. No candy.

Linda's stories appear in many anthologies, including the White City Press anthologies *A Killing at the Copa, Sex & Violins, Gag Me With a Spoon*, and *The Perp Wore Pumpkin*. She's a member of Horror Writers Association, Short Mystery Fiction Society, Queer Crime Writers, Society of Children's Book Writers & Illustrators, and Cat Writers Association. Linda is an Abyssinian Rescue Ranger, volunteering in purebred cat rescue. She works as a writer, writing coach, teddy bear builder, and staff serving purebred rescue cats.

Sandra Murphy lives in St Louis and spends much of her time communing with her imaginary friends who tell her their stories. Unlike guests who eventually leave, imaginary friends stay forever with an endless number of tales to share. Sandra also writes magazine articles, edits a newsletter, and may someday hear a story that will reach book length. Sandra is the editor of the White City Press anthologies *Sex & Violins* and *Yeet Me In St. Louis*, as well as the author of the crime short story collection *From Hay to Eternity*.

Karen Keeley first fell in love with a good who-done-it when she stumbled upon Rex Stout and his *Nero Wolfe* novels at a used bookstore in northwestern Ontario, what she lovingly calls her Archie books. She is the author of "Sticks and Stones, three murder mysteries," and; "There Goes the Neighbourhood, Syd Malloy, Private Investigator, short stories." Her short fiction has appeared in anthologies published by Sisters in Crime—Canada West; Celestial Echo Press; Gutter Books; Outcast Press; Last Waltz Publishing; Black Beacon Books; and many others. A proud Canuck living north of the 49th parallel, she divides her time between family, friends, the outdoors, and writing—not necessarily in that order. Karen appears in the White City Press anthologies *A Killing at the Copa* and *Sex and Violins*.

Teresa Inge is an award-winning mystery author. Her work appears in anthologies and novellas including *First Comes Love, Then Comes Murder* and *Gag Me with a Spoon*.
She is a member of Sisters in Crime, Short Mystery Fiction Society, and Virginia Writer's Club, and she blogs regularly on Sand in our Shorts and Writers Who Kill.
Teresa grew up reading Nancy Drew mysteries. Combining her love of reading mysteries and writing professional articles led to writing crime fiction. By day, she works for a global financial firm as an admin assistant, corporate reporter, and notary administrator. When not writing, she shows her 1955 Torch Red Thunderbird at car shows.

She lives in Southeastern Virginia with her husband and mixed-shepherd Luke and can be reached at www.teresainge.com

Michael Bracken (www.CrimeFictionWriter.com) is the Edgar Award, and Shamus Award-nominated, Derringer-winning author of almost thirteen hundred short stories, including crime fiction published in *Alfred Hitchcock's Mystery Magazine, Ellery Queen's Mystery Magazine, The Best American Mystery Stories, The Best Mystery Stories of the Year,* and many other publications. Additionally, Bracken is the editor of *Black Cat Mystery Magazine* and editor or co-editor of thirty-two published and forthcoming anthologies, including *Janie's Got a Gun: Crime Fiction Inspired by the Music of Aerosmith,* the Anthony Award-nominated *The Eyes of Texas: Private Eyes from the Panhandle to the Piney Woods,* and, with Barb Goffman, the Derringer Award-winning *Murder, Neat.* He is a recipient of the Edward D. Hoch Memorial Golden Derringer Award for lifetime achievement in short mystery fiction and, in 2024, he was inducted into the Texas Institute of Letters for his contributions to Texas literature. He lives, writes, and edits in Texas.

Mary Dutta is the winner of the New England Crime Bake Al Blanchard Award for her short story *The Wonderworker,* which appears in Masthead: Best New England Crime Stories. Her work can also be found in numerous anthologies including the Anthony-nominated Land of 10,000 Thrills: Bouchercon Anthology 2022 and Malice Domestic 16: Mystery Most Diabolical. She is a member of Sisters in Crime and the Short Mystery Fiction Society. Visit her at www.marydutta.com and enjoy her blog at Writers Who Kill. Mary also appears in the White City Press anthology *First Comes Love, Then Comes Murder.*

Nikki Knight is the pen name of Kathleen Marple Kalb, an author/anchor/mom…not in that order. A Regional Edward R. Murrow award-winning weekend anchor at New York's 1010 WINS Radio, she writes mysteries historical and contemporary, long and short, including the Vermont Radio series. Her short stories have appeared in *Alfred Hitchcock's Mystery Magazine, Mystery Magazine, Black Cat Weekly*, in anthologies including *The Perp Wore Pumpkin* and *The Great British Bump-Off* from White City Press, and on short lists for Derringer and Black Orchid Novella Awards. She and her family live in a Connecticut house owned by a large calico cat.

Adam Meyer is a Derringer Award-winning and Shamus Award-nominated author whose short fiction has appeared in *Prohibition Peepers, Mickey Finn, Three Strikes, You're Dead* and other anthologies. He is also the editor of *In Too Deep: Crime Stories Inspired by the Songs of Genesis* and the author of the novel *The Last Domino*. His screenwriting credits include TV series and movies for Lifetime, A&E, National Geographic, and others.